CASTRO VALLEY, CA 94552
USA

Underground Man

Underground Man

MILTON MELTZER

AN ODYSSEY/HARCOURT YOUNG CLASSIC

HARCOURT, INC.

Orlando Austin New York San Diego Toronto London

Copyright © 1972 by Milton Meltzer
Afterword copyright © 1990 by Milton Meltzer

All rights reserved. No part of this publication may be reproduced
or transmitted in any form or by any means, electronic or mechanical,
including photocopy, recording, or any information storage and retrieval system,
without permission in writing from the publisher.

Requests for permission to make copies of any part of the work should be mailed
to the following address: Permissions Department, Harcourt, Inc.,
6277 Sea Harbor Drive, Orlando, Florida 32887-6777.

www.HarcourtBooks.com

First Harcourt Young Classics edition 2006
First Gulliver Books edition 1990
First Odyssey Classics edition 1990
First published by Bradbury Press in 1972

The Library of Congress has cataloged an earlier edition as follows:
Meltzer, Milton, 1915–
Underground man/by Milton Meltzer.
p. cm.
"An Odyssey/Harcourt Young Classic."
Reprint. Originally published: Scarsdale, NY:
Bradbury Press, 1972.
Summary: A courageous young white man aids slaves
escaping from Kentucky in pre–Civil War days.
[1. Underground railroad—Fiction. 2. Slavery—Fiction.] I. Title.
PZ7.M5165Un 1990
[Fic]—dc20 90-36277
ISBN-13: 978-0-15-205518-9 ISBN-10: 15-205518-5
ISBN-13: 978-0-15-205524-0 (pb) ISBN 0-15-205524-X (pb)

Printed in the United States of America

A C E G H F D B
A C E G H F D B (pb)

For Ruth and Ralph Shikes

CONTENTS

Underground Man

1

The Bear

The early morning mist was rising from the swamp when Joshua Bowen heard the dogs faintly in the distance.

"Only two of them," his father said. "Hear that deep holler? And that sharp little yelp?" He put a hand on Rove's head, patting it gently as his dog began to snarl. The brutal sound rumbled in the great chest. Josh felt the skin on the back of his neck prickle. Rove drew back his lips, and the spit began dripping from his mouth.

Preacher Axley stood quietly a moment, head cocked to the west. The Bowens were on their way to the meeting house with the preacher, to build a fire before the Sunday service started. Their path went through the woods bordering the swamp.

"Wonder what they're after?" the preacher said. "Damn if they tree a bear and me without my gun!"

It was Josh who had the only gun—his father's, the old single-barreled flintlock that had taken Mr. Bowen through the War of 1812. It was the one thing his father would not leave behind when they crossed from Massachusetts into New York looking for land to farm in the upstate wilderness. He always took the gun with him when he left the cabin.

"You carry it, Josh," he had said this time. Then, with an edge to his voice, "It isn't loaded."

Josh had taken the gun and tucked it under his arm, the barrel slanting downward. It was the same gun his father had taught him to shoot with when he was ten. That was six years ago. He had learned how all right, but he quit as soon as his father was satisfied he could hit what he aimed at.

"Don't you want a gun of your own?" his father had asked for the hundredth time.

"Let him alone, Fletch," the preacher had said. "You like to hunt. What if the boy doesn't?"

Josh was always glad when Jacob Axley stayed with them. He was the only man Josh knew who could tease his father without its starting a fight.

If only our own preacher would get sick or go away, Josh thought. Then maybe Jacob Axley would stop riding the circuit and settle down right here in Pike.

Suddenly there was a new sound, a growl that seemed to rumble up out of the bowels of the swamp. It hung heavy in the air for seconds, then was broken by the baying of hounds and the crash of undergrowth. Rove tore from his father's side and was almost into the swamp when a great bear lumbered out of it followed by two dogs. One was lean and rangy, the other a stubby little mongrel. They kept close to the bear, running up and snapping at his hindparts when he clambered over logs. But as soon as he turned to slap at them they broke and fell back.

In seconds Rove was at the head of the pack, nipping recklessly at the bear, moving with incredible speed. The bear reared up on his hind legs, waving his huge paws in the air, turning his head warily from one side to the other as the dogs leaped back and forth, barking and biting.

"I bet that's the bear that killed our pig last night!" said Josh. It hadn't been the first time they had lost a pig.

"My gun," his father said. "Give me the gun." Josh handed it over quickly and took the ax from his father.

The noise of the dogs and the growling of their quarry made a great racket in the woods. The bear headed for a large pine, with everyone racing after him. By the time they reached the tree, the bear was high up, hugging the trunk. He looked down at them below. Josh's father stood on one side with his gun, and Jacob Axley on the other, the dogs leaping and barking around them. Something made Rove mad at the bigger dog, and he started fighting with him. Josh saw the bear turning his head from side to side, as though he were figuring out a way to escape. Loosing his hold, he slid down the tree stern foremost, almost as quick as his weight would have brought him had he fallen. Bark and branches fountained in the air as his nails slashed down the trunk.

Josh, his heart hammering rapidly, shrank back several steps. His father was holding the gun to his shoulder, but, suddenly remembering it wasn't loaded, he turned it and held it like a club. He glanced around for Josh and, seeing where he was standing, angrily waved him closer to the tree.

There was no time to be afraid. A thunderous thump—Josh could feel the ground tremble—and the bear was down on his side of the tree. A hot, rank smell came from the shaggy hulk. The dogs moved in swiftly. He raised the ax, hesitated, felt his father's eyes burning into him, swung with all his might just as Rove's body jetted through the air. The ax struck deep into Rove's neck. The dog sank to the earth, the wound gaping wide. He shuddered once and then was still. Josh dropped the ax and stood with his hands over his face, sobbing.

"Damn you!" his father cried. He shoved Josh aside roughly and knelt beside Rove. "Dead," he said in a flat voice, looking up at the preacher.

The preacher had moved to Josh's side and was holding him with one arm around his shoulders. "Come on, Fletch," he said. "We've got to get the bear. We can't let him get away. He'll do too much harm."

The bear had run off toward the swamp, changed his mind, and headed for another pine with the dogs tight on his heels. Up and up he climbed until he was fifty feet above the ground, resting with his neck partly over a branch.

Josh's father stood up, ignoring Josh. He took some buckshot out, tore off a rag and wrapped as many shot in it as he could force down the barrel. It made a sort of cartridge that would keep the shot closer together when the gun was fired. Then he primed it with fresh powder.

"The throat," he said, as they moved toward the pine tree. "That'll finish him."

He circled the tree till he found the best angle. The gun roared, and this time, instead of falling with dead weight, the bear seemed to float out into space like an old rug and, turning end over end, flattened at last on the ground. Astonishingly, he was up and off in a moment, the dogs yelling after him. The blood gushed from his torn throat and seventy-five yards off he staggered as though hit again, and crumpled into the pine needles.

2

Father and Son

"Josh, you go on into the village to get a team so we can bring the bear in. I'll stay here," his father said, motioning toward Rove. "Will you go with him, Jacob?"

The preacher looked at Josh. The boy was crouched by the huge hulk, but his eyes were fixed in the distance, where Rove lay.

"No," the preacher said, "I'll wait here."

Josh got up slowly. He passed by his father and hesitated, wanting to speak to him. Mr. Bowen turned his head away. Josh walked off in the direction of the village.

Mr. Bowen picked up the ax. The crimson stains on the blade were already turning brown and crusting. He chopped out a patch of the undergrowth, then dug a shallow hole in the earth while Jacob Axley watched. It was plain he wanted to do this by himself. When the grave was big enough, he picked up Rove in his arms and carried him to it. The big body was so heavy and stiff it was awkward to lower it, and the preacher helped him. Then they pushed the dirt over the dog until a slight mound was raised. They found some rocks and piled them on top.

All during the burial Mr. Bowen worked silently. When they were finished, he sat against a tree and lit his pipe. He stared off into the gray woods.

"Fletch?"

"Don't need to say it."

"Say what?"

"That I'm hard on the boy."

The preacher was quiet. Then, "I know how you feel about Rove. But Josh isn't to blame. I could have done it, or even you. It happens."

"That's not it, Jacob. I know he didn't try to kill the dog."

"Then why are you so angry?"

"He's scared, Jacob, the boy's scared. Scared of the bear. You saw that. Scared of Rove. Always was. Couldn't stand to be near him."

"Nor could anyone else, Fletcher—you know that! Rove was mean. You were the only living thing he'd tolerate."

"But Josh was even scared of a pig, Jacob. A

pig! Years back—it wasn't much after he took over the chore of feeding the pigs—we had a big hog, biggest one in the drove. A selfish brute, he was. Always out to have everything for himself. But that's a hog for you. Josh, he couldn't stand him. Thought he was cruel to the little ones. A pig, cruel!

"One day the hog got mad when Josh kept trying to prod him away from the trough. He turned on the boy, and Josh streaked it out of the pen. Went flying right over the rail. Then, I don't know what got into him, he caught up a stone and flung it at the hog. Hit him right in the face. The poor animal screamed and ran around the pen like a madman. Finally he stopped, lay down and began to moan. Then Josh saw what he had done. He'd knocked out the hog's eye. The boy couldn't sleep. He kept waking up with nightmares, said he saw the empty socket and the eye hanging below it on a cord. It was weeks before he'd sleep through the night."

"Tell me, Fletcher, you never been scared?"

"Not so's anybody would notice."

"Then you were scared!"

"Well, in the war I was. But wasn't another soldier who could tell."

"So it isn't being scared that riles you. It's *showing* it."

"Jacob, the boy's like a woman that way. They got feelings, and they have to let you know about em. In a woman I can take that. But not in a man."

"Fletcher, you're a fool sometimes. Josh is no coward. It's just that he doesn't pocket his feelings. You have some damn-fool notion of what a real man is."

"Don't come off telling me how to raise a boy, Jacob! You ever done it? You ain't even tried getting married!"

The preacher laughed. "Aw shut up," he said.

The team of oxen were coming up now. With a sledge they dragged the bear out of the woods and brought it into Pierce's tavern, close by the meeting house. Convenient it was for those worshippers who liked a nip and a chance to talk over farm affairs after the service.

The whole congregation was waiting for them. Mr. Pierce brought out his rum and gave the company a treat, not forgetting himself. The bear, his skin pulled off, was soon butchered and distributed.

It was hours after the morning service should have begun. Preacher Axley leaped up on a barrel and announced there would be no service today.

"It's a good Christian act to destroy a dangerous animal on the Sabbath," he said. "It may not be exactly within the canons of the church, mind you, but 'tis a venial offense. The Lord will overlook it."

A cheer went up. The preacher raised his mug to the congregation, bowed, took a deep swallow and got down.

They rode home in the wagon Josh's mother had driven in to church. Josh took the reins, his mother sitting beside him. He'd known at once that she had heard what happened in the woods. When he'd helped her into the wagon she had given his arm a tight squeeze. As they sat down she had leaned over and kissed him lightly on the cheek.

The wagon jolted over the ruts. In the back, the preacher kept asking about this member of the congregation and that, getting only a grunt out of Josh's father beside him. It was his mother who did all the answering. She knew everything about everyone in that church.

They talked in a carefully casual way, as though trying to avoid anything that would be upsetting. The voices became only scattered noise in Josh's ear. He was thinking how Rove would have been scouting before the wagon now, the way he used to every Sunday on the way to and from service. He'd clear the road of hens, geese, pigs and cattle, terrifying those slow to move with his deep growl. While

11

they were sitting in church he'd wait, lying in the bed of the wagon, snarling when any stranger approached.

When would his father say something about Rove? Was he going to wait and wait and wait again? Josh had never forgotten the time he broke one of his father's rules and expected to be whipped for it. It was so long ago it was hard to remember exactly what he had done at school that was forbidden. But he had told his father as soon as he got home that day, set in his mind for the usual whipping. His father listened to him quietly but all evening said not one word about it. He was busy packing up for the long journey to Albany; Josh bustled around, helping him all he could, and this his father let him do, but in a cool way that was ominous. Josh went to bed without the whipping, tossing all night with worry.

The next morning he got up early to see his father off. They all had breakfast together, the horse was saddled and at the door and still not one word about the whipping. Josh could not suppose for a moment that he had forgotten it, for he saw the whip in that tight-set face and heard it in that deliberate voice.

When everything was ready, his father went to the door, Josh tagging close behind. He vaulted on his horse, picked up the reins and, looking down, whispered in an icy tone, "Josh, I'll settle with you when I come back."

Then he rode off.

For two weeks the torture lasted. Josh could hardly sleep or eat. A dozen whippings would have been better than this suspense. Every day the anxiety built higher in him, like a fever. At last his father returned, and as soon as he came into the house Josh begged him to get it over with. His father knew just what he meant. And did it.

That night, from his bed in the loft, Josh heard his mother pleading: "Couldn't you understand how you were torturing that boy? For God's sake, Fletcher, take him as he is!"

He never struck Josh again.

Instead, when he got mad, he locked himself up in long silences worse than any whipping.

Now the wagon was pulling up to the house, and everyone got busy with the chores and preparing for supper. Jacob Axley ate so much of the bear meat they feared he'd get sick. No one blamed him for his appetite. Preachers riding the circuit ate badly, and sometimes not at all. And Jacob was huge. His head was half a bushel big.

They were having their coffee when his father suddenly turned to Josh.

"Josh, you'll be seventeen come next birthday?"

"He will," his mother put in, "and you know that as well as anyone."

"I'm not asking you, Betsey." He took out his pipe and lit it. "What do you plan to do? You're pretty much a man now."

Josh was startled. What did he plan to do? Why nothing, nothing but what he had been doing—the chores on the farm, going to school in the winter months—what else was there to do? Get married some day and start a family? He wasn't in any hurry for that.

"I don't know, Pa. What do you mean?"

"Don't you want to get about in the world? See something besides Pike? There's a lot besides this out there," he said, waving an arm vaguely toward some unknown horizon.

"Well, sure, Pa, and I will some day. But there's so much to do around the farm. You need me."

Josh's mother was sitting stiff in her chair. "What are you getting at, Fletcher?" she said. The preacher shifted uncomfortably in his seat, put his hand over his big belly and groaned.

"Why, only that I think it's time Josh learned a trade, something useful he can make a living at."

"I thought the farm was that, Pa. Are you planning to sell it or something?"

"No," his father said, "I'm not."

On her feet, voice crackling, Mrs. Bowen said, "Fletcher, come out with it. You've already done something and not told any of us about it. What is it?"

"Calm down, Betsey," he said. "Nothing to be so angry about. I've been talking to Dave Folsom—you know, the hatmaker over at Hornell? He says he'll be glad to take on an apprentice."

A sourness flooded up into Josh's mouth. He tried to speak but his mother was too quick.

"A hatter's apprentice? What for, in God's name? Here are good fat acres that badly need more hands, and you're sending Josh away! You're daft!"

A flush spread slowly over Mr. Bowen's face. "It's not such a crazy notion, Betsey," he said, keeping his voice under control. "It makes sense if you look at it right. But as usual you won't let the boy speak for himself. I want to know what Josh thinks."

They were all looking at him now. Through the window he could see the sun suspended low in the west, orange-red before it dropped suddenly out of sight. A last brilliant ray beamed across his father's face. The green eyes blinked, then the sun was gone. The room darkened swiftly. His mother lit a lamp and set it on the table. He noticed that her usually steady hands trembled.

"Think, Pa? I don't know what to think. The idea just never occurred to me. Making hats?" My father wants to get rid of me, he thought. For killing a dog.

The preacher intervened, trying to give Josh time to pull himself together, "How long an apprenticeship would it be, Fletcher?"

"Folsom says four years. He'll draw up indentures for him and me to sign. It'd bind Josh till he's twenty-one."

"But he's never been away from home," his mother said. "Not more than a day at a time."

"If you're thinking he'll be lonely, there's no need to fear. I saw several journeymen and apprentices in Folsom's shop. Josh wouldn't be the only one. He'll have more company his own age than he does here at home. And Hornell's a lot bigger place than Pike."

"But Pa!" Josh's throat was dry now, the words coming out hoarse. "I don't want to be a hatter!"

"That may be," his father said. "But you are no farmer."

Josh was stunned. No farmer! what else was he? What had he been doing since he could lift a milking pail or hold a plow? The blood hammered in his head.

"What are you saying, Fletcher!" His mother

was talking. "Josh will be just as much a farmer as you are, and your father was, and mine! What kind of farmer are you talking about?"

Mr. Bowen's face tightened. He had made up his mind to something. "What I mean is, sure, he'll run this place with me around, and maybe run it after I'm gone. But he won't run it well. He can't. He ain't the man for it."

Josh cut in before his mother could get out the next word. "Pa, you're not forgiving me because I killed Rove. You know it was an accident! But you won't even let me say I'm sorry! I've tried, but when I look at you, it's stone I see, not a face. That dog—you cared more about—" He couldn't say it.

"It isn't that, Josh. Not just that," his father said. "Some people are born for the land. The others—oh, they can learn how to work it when they have to. But they never feel it the way a farmer does. Maybe they don't know what else to do, maybe they never get a chance to find out. So they stick with it till it's too late."

"That's true, Josh," said the preacher. "It took a long time for me to find it out. I was over thirty before I realized it was something else I needed, not the land. And the Lord knows, it isn't just a matter of being happy. What's 'happy'? Is that what it's about? It's more the feeling you get that what you are fits with what you're doing. It's finding the right key to turn the lock. Don't know but that many people never find it."

"Whose business you minding now?" said Josh, turning on Jacob. "You don't know what you're talking about, no more than him. How does he know what I feel about anything? Does he ever ask me? Does he ever talk to me?"

"Josh, Josh, please!" said his mother, her hand on his arm, trying to quiet him.

He pushed her off roughly.

His father jumped up, grabbed him by the shoulders. "What are you doing, boy! Don't you touch your mother like that. Better say you're sorry! Right now!"

Josh twisted out of his father's grasp. "I'm sorry, all right, sorry I got a father like you! Can't hardly talk, less you got orders to give. Do this, do that, go here, go there, this is right, that's wrong. But a human word? No, I never hear one—"

The heavy hand swept through the air, and the back of it cracked across Josh's mouth. There was a thick, strangled sound as though Josh's tongue had been shoved down his throat. He fell back against the wall, his hands covering his eyes. He leaned there a moment, gasping for breath. Then he turned and groped for the stairs, lifting himself slowly, step by step, to his room in the loft.

3

A True Calling?

Before dawn the next day Josh was up to see the preacher off. He fed Jacob's horses in the barn, then saddled them. Axley weighed all of 250 pounds and needed two horses to carry him on his long journeys. He rode one till it got tired, then switched to the other.

It was not yet light when Jacob came clumping down from the loft.

"Where your folks?" he asked.

Josh nodded toward the closed door. "Still asleep, I guess."

They sat on stools before the fire Josh had built, sharing coffee and bread.

"You don't feel so good this morning, boy."

Josh drew a deep breath. He ran his hand through his coarse black hair, which shot out in all directions like a porcupine's quills.

The preacher sighed. "Your pa's a good man, Josh. He don't mean to hurt you."

"No?"

"He's clumsy, that's what it is."

"That's no word for it."

"I mean clumsy with people, Josh. Fletcher's fine with things, with the land, with dumb beasts. They tell me he made a great rifleman. But with people? That's much harder. They're not like a gun you can take apart to clean and put together, every little piece in its place, oiled and ready for use again. The parts don't fit so easy in a man. Sometimes a part's missing, and still it works."

"Are you talking about Pa or me?"

"About any of us," said the preacher. He looked down the great length of leg stretched out to the fire and, raising his cup for another splash of coffee, asked, "Josh, is it farming you want to do?"

"I thought so! But then when Pa said, 'You're no farmer,' I had a terrible feeling—my head was so mixed up. One part of me felt of course I was; Pa's crazy to say that. But inside me something said, maybe he's right! And I was relieved to hear it said, Jacob! Angry, ready to hit him, and at the same time, glad."

The preacher laughed.

And then Josh laughed, too. "Funny thing," he said, "I feel all up in the air, and I'm laughing. It's so crazy the way things come about." He got up to poke the fire and, turning to the preacher, said, "But what am I going to do?"

"That you'll have to answer for yourself, Josh. I don't think your pa is going to throw you out of the house."

They went outside. The sun was filtering light through the treetops. The woods stood silent except for the faint rustling of dry leaves in the wind. The barberry bushes were alive with robins feeding on their scarlet fruit.

"Ah," the preacher said, "these woods. I'm glad this world isn't all man. I think I'd lose hope."

"I thought you were content," Josh said.

"Right here and now I am. But out there—in the villages, the cities—sometimes they make me wish for another world. These lichens on the rocks, they seem more my own kith and kin than those churchgoers in the pews."

"Then why did you leave the farm?"

"Not because I didn't love the land, Josh. Maybe it was the endless round of chores. By the time I was thirty I felt sentenced for life to the plow. My father started the farm, and at first it was just to take care of his own family. But he couldn't help making it bigger and bigger. It wasn't food we were raising any more; it was crops of dollar bills. Life flows with a deeper current than that, Josh." The preacher climbed up on one of his horses, tying a rope from the other to his saddle. "I think we were made to rejoice, not drown in the sweat of our brow."

The preacher bent down and held out his hand to Josh. Then he rode off slowly into the dark evergreen.

Josh turned and saw his mother standing in the doorway, watching Jacob disappear in the distance.

"Have coffee with me, son?"

"I've had mine, with Jacob."

"Then just keep me company?"

He gave in. He sat opposite her, fiddling with a spoon, his eyes fixed on the table. He could feel her watching him.

"Josh, you'll stay, won't you?"

"Why should I? He doesn't want me to."

"Don't believe that," she said. "He won't bring up Folsom again. I promise you that."

"It doesn't matter. I wouldn't become a hatter even if he tried to force me. But I can't stay here either. Not now."

"But you don't have to go off without knowing to where or to what. There's plenty of time to decide."

"He doesn't think so. Always reminding me how he was in the army by this time."

"Why compare yourself to him? What if he was?

He's Fletcher Bowen and you're Joshua Bowen. You're not one and the same. Why should you be?"

"You know good and well the last thing on earth I want to be is him!"

"Josh! I didn't mean it that way. It's just that we're all different, and thank God for it. Who'd want a world with every one of us as alike as peas in a pod?"

"Especially if it was Pa's pod," he said.

She laughed. "Josh, ever thought about going into the church?"

"Me? A preacher? Forget it, Ma. I'll come to whatever it is by myself."

The bedroom door opened behind him with a sudden, emphatic jerk. He wondered if his father had been listening. No, he couldn't have cared less what Josh thought. His father went over to the stove and poured himself some coffee. He wouldn't look at Josh.

"Morning, Fletcher," his mother said. "Sit down. Let me fry up some bacon."

"I'm late," he said. "Got to get out to the barn. This'll do for now."

Every morning he'd walk down to the barn with Josh, and they'd start the chores together. This time, he started for the door alone.

"All right. Josh'll be along in a minute."

His father grunted and went out.

"Go ahead, Josh," she said.

He sat there, not moving. She reached across the table to touch his hand. He stood up abruptly, took his jacket from the peg on the wall, and went out after his father. In the barn he found him sharpening an ax. "The milking," his father said, "get started on that."

They always did it together. Josh liked that, even though his father rarely said anything while they worked. It was plain now that he expected Josh to do it alone. All day his father assigned him chores Josh could do by himself. Once, when a heavy rock had to be shifted, his father struggled to do it alone, then motioned Josh to help. While they worked with the crowbars, Josh became aware his father was looking at him guardedly. When Josh caught his eye, his father glanced down. He wants to say something, Josh thought. Doesn't know how to start. The rock stirred at last, they heaved together, and it rolled out of the way. By late afternoon Josh was carrying on such intense conversations with his father in his head that he felt the words must surely be heard.

"Pa," he burst out, "don't expect me to beg!"

"For what?" his father said.

"To stay here, dammit!"

"Who's asking you to go? Do as you like. All I did was tell you Folsom had a place for you. And you take on like a lunatic."

"Me!"

His father put down the harness he had been repairing.

"You," he said. He stood up. "I don't want to talk about this any more. You don't like what I do, you don't have to. You want to stay here, stay. Your ma and me, we brought you into this world—"

"Who asked to be born," Josh muttered.

"Don't say that! I know it was a bad beginning, but that's God's way—so your mother says."

His father had often reminded him of it. The crazy weather the summer Josh was born. Snow falling in June and frosts in July and August killing the buckwheat and corn. Living—starving rather—on roots and herbs, and Josh's birth coming months ahead of time. His mother so weak the effort nearly killing her. "What a miserable creature for the first-born!" He could see his father standing over the birthing bed, could hear him think it. He knew why his mother couldn't have more children.

"At least she thinks it was God's fault, not mine!"

His father's hands trembled. Then, in a slow, measured tone he said, "For a little man, you got one hell of a big mouth."

Josh stared at him, eyes burning, heart pounding, the taste of hatred in his mouth.

Josh woke to the sound of hooves on the hard ground, coming muffled through the layers of leaves that had already fallen from the November trees. Two horses, not one. And now he could tell that only one carried a rider.

He threw on pants and shirt and was outside the door before Jacob Axley could dismount.

"Josh," the preacher said, reaching down and giving the clump of black hair a gentle tug. "Two months since I've seen you. Don't look hardly any older, nor wiser." Josh laughed and took the reins to lead the horses to the barn. They needed to be fed and watered. The preacher had ridden through most of the night. "I'm only stopping a few hours," he said. "They expect me up north by tomorrow."

"How about some breakfast?" Josh asked, concealing his disappointment.

"Not right now, Josh. I ate a bit on the trail. It can wait." He stretched his powerful arms above his head and yawned. "Stiff from all those hours in the saddle. Let's walk a little first."

They headed toward the swamp, moving through a blaze of maples and hickories and scarlet oaks. Beneath their feet the fallen pine needles were shining green above the brown earth. The preacher reached into his pocket and found two apples. They bit into the juicy sweetness. Off the path to the left was an oak lot that Josh had helped his father cut. They sat down on stumps. A hawk screamed in the sky, and they watched it wheeling lazily. The preacher munched his apple core, spitting out the seeds.

"Jacob, I've been wondering about how you came into the church. Ma's talked to me about it. Was it preaching you took up as soon as you quit the farm?"

"Not at first, Josh. I wanted to see something of the world, something different." He paused and flung the core into the woods. "Didn't find out much except what a beautiful world this is and what miserable people we are that live in it. When I got back home I saw my own village as though for the first time. Traveling rubbed off my rust. I went a long way from home only to get closer to it."

"But you didn't stay."

"No, I didn't like farming any better than before. Nor the way my father thought it was superior. Farming's all right, but is it any more the real business of life than the other ways men get their living?"

"But what's so superior about preaching, Jacob?

My God, that preacher Mr. Holman in our meeting house—you know him!—he has no more life in him than this dried-up old stick. All smug and smirk, he is. Only time that man shows any feelings is when he goes hell-and-damnation on us."

The preacher laughed. "That's the very thing, Josh. It was the Holmans that drove me into the church. They crawl around like worms in the shell of Christianity. Little of the divine is left in it. Our preacher back home was no different from your Mr. Holman. I used to sit there and wonder how we could all endure to listen to a minister who knew nothing of God's meaning when we would never have sat through the singing of a man who had no ear for music."

"Me too, Jacob! Ma got so mad when I said I couldn't imagine that if the saints came to earth again, they would stay at Mr. Holman's house."

"Josh," he said with mock solemnity, "you are ready to become a preacher."

"What do you mean?"

"I mean that when a man knows the church needs life restored to it, he's the man to do it."

"But I don't know anything about it . . . I never thought . . ." He heard his own words protesting, then cut them off abruptly. Why not?

"Jacob"—he was asking it slowly for fear the answer would not be what he wanted to hear— "Jacob, you aren't fooling about this; you do mean it, you do think maybe I could learn to preach, could learn from *you?*"

"Josh, seventeen or not, you're a man. You do what you want to do. If you feel called to travel in God's service, then do it."

Suddenly he was doubtful. "Called? I think maybe I feel the spirit. But I've had no visions, no revelations."

"No one asks a miracle of you, Joshua."

"And I'm a sinner, too. I've done terrible things, wished terrible things on others."

"So have all of us, Josh. Sin is nothing but selfishness. Thinking only about our own desires is what leads us to do wrong. Holiness—what is it? It's having feeling for others, respect for them, for our fellow man. Any sinner can have a new heart. But he must make it himself. It takes no miracle of the Holy Ghost."

"You don't sound like Mr. Holman."

"That I don't. Nor will you ever. And you have another advantage over him, Josh."

"What's that?"

"You look like something. Small, to be sure,

but they'll see your head over the pulpit. And the women will like what they see. Of course, you'll have to comb your hair once in a while."

Josh was pleased.

"Your voice'll surprise people. It's about twice as deep as you're high. That's good. A squeaky preacher drives em crazy."

Josh's mother was overjoyed when they told her. "We are giving our only son to the church," she said.

"It may be only a short loan," the preacher cautioned.

"No, he's going for good. I feel it."

Fletcher Bowen was skeptical. "This sudden conversion, Jacob, how long will it last?"

"No more sudden than mine," the preacher answered. "I was bringing in the corn one afternoon, and the next morning I was gone. Seemed sudden, even to me. But the seed was growing a long time before it sprouted. Josh too. Whether he'll stay with the ministry or not, I can't promise. But he's not for the farm, Fletcher, and you knew it before all of us."

"But what if he finds this isn't his true calling?"

"What if? He won't die of it. He's not being condemned for life. It's the church, Fletcher, not a penitentiary."

4

Riding the Circuit

Come hungry, come thirsty,
come ragged, come bare,
Come filthy, come lousy,
come just as you are

The old revival tune boomed through the trees as the two circuit riders jogged along the narrow trail to the campground. The preacher was in front and Josh in the rear. When the weather was fine and their bellies filled, they liked to try close harmony. No hymn, this, but Jacob Axley was not a man to shut his ears to a good tune.

It was spring now. Josh saw the catkins of the willow gleaming silver. New flowers were unfolding fast, although some of the ponds they passed still showed ice. He heard the clear loud warble of a finch and off to the left saw it sitting purple on an elm.

His eyes settled on the broad back jolting up and down in front of him. A year, the church fathers had given him, a year to prove himself a preacher, under Jacob Axley's wing. It was nearly six months since they had started out on the circuit together. It was a hard school. Jacob took his charge seriously. "The circuit's your true college," he had said. "Educate yourself."

In the saddlebags was their library. Bible and hymnbook first of all. The works of John Wesley, a scattering of doctrinal tracts. "That's to prime you," the preacher had said. "But no apprentice of mine gets by just with that." And he'd pulled out another batch of books. The Koran—"to keep up with the competition." He relished its poetry the way he did the Old Testament's. Cooper's novel, *The Prairie*; a Greek and Roman history; Webster's *Dictionary*, Washington Irving's *Sketch Book*, and a new book by Lydia Maria Child, *An Appeal for That Class of Americans Called Africans*.

Jacob insisted every spare moment be given to reading. They rose at five to study before breakfast, no matter where they were. Often the horses moved very slowly on the trails, and they read while jerking along in the saddle. He was lucky, Josh knew, that Jacob Axley had an unbounded appetite for learning. The preacher had mastered the gospel long ago, but he had also mastered carpentry, shoemaking and veterinary medicine. He taught Josh navigation by dead reckoning and set him problems to solve in mathematics and geometry.

Jacob's salary was $100 a year, Josh's not half that. Nor did they always get it. Often they lay out in the woods all night, cold, tired and hungry. They slept with saddle blanket for bed, saddle for pillow, and coat (when they had one) for covering. They ate roasting ears for bread and drank buttermilk for coffee, or sage tea. For breakfast, dinner and supper it was deer or bear meat—when they could get it. They had to beg oats and corn for their horses.

Josh's first winter on the circuit had been a misery of driving rains and heavy snows. Only two weeks ago, this spring landscape had seemed impossible. And now the blowing wind, strong but warm, was whetting senses that had been sleeping like the earth. The very grain of the air seemed to have changed.

It was night when they reached the revival campground. Methodists from thirty or forty miles around were streaming in by wagon or buggy, on horseback or on foot, bringing their tents, beds and provisions. The tents were set up amid the trees surrounding the clearing. Here the men, women and children would live for four or five days, sometimes several families in a tent.

Josh and Jacob put up their horses near the tent set aside for the preachers and then wandered about, greeting old friends. The bright watch fires and candles inside the enclosure made the dark of the forest even gloomier. On the edge of the camp were the gingerbread and whisky carts. Every night the noise of drunken revelry outside rose in the air to mingle in confusion with the singing and preaching inside. "God and the devil," Jacob had said the first time Josh saw it. "Inseparable." The guzzlers didn't bother him. "If there were no sinners," he would say, "there'd be no saints."

By this time the crowd, grown huge, was plunged into prayers. The uproar filled Josh's head like a clanging alarm bell. The shouting, the singing, the crying out for mercy, never ceased. From the platform he watched preacher after preacher exhort the crowd to let the Lord Omnipotent reign in their hearts. Submit to Him, they begged, so that your soul shall live.

There were hymns now, rocking the crowd ever higher, and then it was Jacob's turn. He began in a simple downright style, but soon his voice rose in a deep-throated shout that penetrated to the far edge of the clearing. For a moment Josh felt the fire building in his bones. "And it shall be for a sign, and for a witness unto the Lord of Hosts in the land of Egypt: for they shall cry unto the Lord because of the oppressors, and He shall send them a Saviour, and a great one, and He shall deliver them." What was Jacob preaching? But Josh had lost the thread. There was that terrific burst of eloquence, and people falling like corn before a storm of wind. He closed his eyes and could see himself standing on the platform, making all the right gestures and saying all the right things. Only it was always like a bad actor's performance, all imitation and no true feeling.

He wanted desperately to preach like Jacob. "Don't copy me," Jacob had said again and again. "Be yourself!" But how? "Stop worrying about style," the preacher said. "You don't learn by standing in front of a looking glass and making motions. Pump yourself full of the spirit till you can't hold another drop, then knock out the bung and let nature caper!" But Josh's preaching was always from the head, not the heart. Jacob shook people to their roots.

Now men, women and children were crying, shouting, groaning, repeating his friend's phrases over and over, faster and faster. And then a thousand voices exploded in a universal shout. But in Josh's ear it was like the roar of Niagara heard miles off, a faint sound infinitely remote from himself. And suddenly he knew he did not belong here on this platform. He was pretending, just pretending. He had heard no call.

Josh slipped away. No one noticed him leave in the tumult that rose and fell like a surging sea. On Jacob's blanket in the tent he left a note: *I'm not ready for this life; maybe I never will be. God be with you, Jacob. I owe you everything. I'm going west.*

To do what? he said to himself as he scrawled the words. He hadn't even known where he was going until he saw the words on the paper.

5

Sam's Story

Josh was poling the raft slowly down the river when he saw a man walking along the Kentucky shore, an ax on his shoulder. The man was about six feet tall and wearing blue cotton pants and a striped shirt. He walked heavily, his head down. As Josh drifted parallel to him, the man lifted his face and looked across the water to the Ohio shore. His skin was a dark chestnut color. When he turned his gaze downriver, Josh saw a scar. It was blue and ran down the left side of his face in a ridge, stopping at the corner of his mouth.

The big raft, made up of logs Josh was floating to a lumber mill, coasted close by the riverbank. The black man on shore increased his pace, as though to keep abreast. He glanced at Josh but said nothing. Now the river path curved inland around a clump of trees, and Josh lost sight of the man. But there he was again, breathing hard. Must have run around the trees so he could catch up with me, Josh thought. The current was sluggish a few minutes later and the raft slowed. So did the man on the bank.

Then Josh hit a snag, jutting rocks that forced one edge of the raft to the shore. It wedged between rock and riverbank. Josh struggled to pole the raft loose, but it was too heavy for him. The black man had stopped to watch. Seeing Josh was losing out, he swiftly chopped a big branch from a tree, trimmed it roughly, and, leaping onto the raft, helped Josh shove it free.

"Where bound?" he asked.

"Skinner's mill."

"But that's on the Ohio side. What you doing along this shore?"

"I thought the current would be swifter here," Josh said. "I thought wrong."

"You surely did," the man said.

"Guess I'm learning the hard way. The logger I've been cutting timber for told me to start rafting the logs down to the mill. Never asked me did I know the river. I wasn't about to tell him I didn't."

"Well," the man said, "it's shallow along here. Uncertain sometimes. But you'll get there all right."

"What about the Ohio side?" Josh asked.

The man shook his head. "Don't know about that. Never been there."

Josh looked surprised.

"Where you from?" the man said.

"York State, I came out here but a few months back."

"Ohhhh," the man said. He was sitting on the raft, his ax between his knees. The green shore eased by. He seemed to be watching it, but then Josh saw that his eyes were blank. Suddenly he sprang to his feet.

"Mister," he said, "will you take a chance?"

"What chance?" said Josh. "What are you talking about?"

"I'm a slave."

Josh was startled. How could he have been so slow-witted? A black man, on the Kentucky side— what else would he most likely be? Josh hadn't come across more than two or three black folk in his part of New York. And they'd been free. Coming out to Ohio, he'd seen many more in the towns. Free people, all of them—at least now. Some, he knew, had been runaway slaves. And instantly he realized what his passenger was coming to.

"No, I didn't know," he said. "I mean, I didn't think about it."

"*Now* you know."

"All right," Josh said. He began poling the raft away from the Kentucky shore. The man crouched down, watching.

Suddenly a horseman broke out of the Kentucky woods and rode down to the riverbank. His horse bent to drink. Josh watched him as he kept poling. The rider looked up and saw the raft. He reined his horse back, rode him a few steps down the shore, as though trying to follow the raft. But its movement was across the river, not up or down. The black man too had seen the rider. Silently he slid off the raft's far edge and, taking a deep breath, submerged himself in the water, clinging to the raft only with his fingertips. Josh dug his pole deep to move the raft faster. Now the horseman was standing still. He rose in his stirrups and shielding his eyes with his hand, stared hard at the raft for a few seconds. Then, seeing nothing but a white man aboard, he pulled his horse about and rode back into the woods just as the black man appeared above the water, gasping for air.

"It's safe now," Josh said. "He's gone." The man pulled himself aboard again and lay flat, face down. He shivered as the wind swept over his wet clothing. As the raft neared the other shore he reached for the pole he had shaped, and together they maneuvered the raft into a cove on the Ohio side. When the logs grounded on the sandy bottom, the man turned his head to look for a long minute toward Kentucky, now only faintly visible in the late afternoon shadows, and then stepped off the raft.

He walked quickly to the nearest tree, leaned his ax against it, and sat down. Josh followed, noticing the man had put himself where he could not be seen from the river.

"My name's Josh Bowen."

"Sam," the black man said.

"Sam . . . ?"

"Got no other name. Just Sam."

It was almost dark now. Josh got up and lashed one end of the raft to a big tree, so it wouldn't drift off in the night. When he came back, Sam was sitting there, digging his fingers into the dirt, then looking at it in the palm of his hand. "Feels the same," he said. "You never been the other side the Ohio?"

"No."

"Don't look much different from this."

"Let's eat," said Josh. "I'm hungry." He got up and took some food from a pouch tied on the raft. They made a small fire. Sam took off his shoes and most of his clothes to dry them by the fire. Josh threw some bacon on to cook. A bubble of fat exploded off the sizzling strip and hit Sam's cheek.

He winced in pain and touched his face. He caught Josh staring at the old scar. "Dogs," he said. "Dogs did that." Suddenly he seemed restless. "I better move on. Don't like staying so close to the river."

"But where will you go?"

"North. I'll head as far north as I can get. Maybe Canada. I hear we free there."

"Here, too," said Josh. "Ohio's a free state."

"You new here," the black man said. "This part of Ohio's full of settlers from the slavery side of the river. Don't like niggers any more 'n folks in Kentucky do. A runaway get caught, they rush him right back across the river. And if they catch you helping a runaway—you not much better off." He hesitated. "That why I wasn't sure about you."

Josh studied Sam across the fire. "You have a family?"

The black man took out a cob, lit it with a coal, and began puffing at it. "I had a wife," he said. "And children. Two of them."

"Where are they now?"

He nodded toward the river. "Back there some place. The Lord only knows where. The children, I lost them first. A long time ago." In bits and pieces he told Josh what had happened. He had lived on the Cabell place in Kentucky. The farmer raised hemp, livestock, a little corn and peas. Old Cabell didn't have much sense, except to marry rich. His wife had all the land and slaves. Sam grew up with a girl named Easter. One day Cabell let a preacher marry them.

Easter had her first baby, and the Cabells put the little boy to work as soon as he could walk. "Our first one—Willie—I remember he held a hoe handle mighty unsteady when Easter showed him how to scrape the fields. She'd work alongside him and then turn about to show some other child, and Willie would have the young corn cut as clean as the grass. 'For the love of God,' she'd tell him, 'you better learn it right or the driver will beat the breath out of you.' "

They made their log cabin as snug as they could—chinked it with a mixture of clay and hog-hair scrapings, slept on mattresses stuffed with moss. Their eating wasn't bad. In hard times Cabell half-rationed the slaves till they weren't much fit for work. But they caught squirrel and quail and had a little patch for potatoes and goobers.

Easter often worked in the spinning house, too. The loom and wheel kept going all the time. She put in such long and hard hours she'd fall asleep at the loom sometimes.

"One day Cabell's boy, he see her sleeping. He go tell his ma. She say take a whip and wear Easter out. The boy come into the cabin with a stick and hit her a whack that woke her up. She snatched a pole out of the loom and beat him. He holler to stop, but she so crazy mad she can't. When her arm too tired to lift any more, that boy not able to walk. My God, she think, they gone kill me. But they do worse. They tell her they gone sell her and sell our children."

"What about you, Sam?"

"Me they keep," he answered bitterly, "cause this nigger too good a head to sell."

Easter went nearly crazy, she told Sam later. That night—she wouldn't ask Sam; she thought he'd try to stop her—she ran off to the woods with the children, hoping to keep them with her that way. She fed the children berries and stolen potatoes and raw corn. They drank water from the ponds and puddles. They were sick with fear and lack of sleep when the patrol found them three days later.

They locked Easter up in a cabin, away from Sam. A few days later Mr. Stone, the slave trader, came by, and the Cabells told him to take the children and Easter away and sell them. Sam was out in the fields. They never saw him to say good-bye.

Sam did not know where his family had gone or who had bought them or if they had been sold together. He figured if he could get away, he might find them somehow. In his grief, not knowing where to look, he ran off to the woods. It wasn't long before he heard the hounds howling in the distance.

"How did the dogs know to find you so fast?"

"They train them," Sam said. "They take pups, any kind of pup will do—foxhounds, bulldogs, most any—and keep em shut up, and don't let em ever see a nigger till the pups get old enough to be set onto things. Then they make em run after a nigger, and when they catch him, they give em meat. They tell the nigger to run hard as he can and get up in a tree, so as to teach the dogs to tree em. They take the shoe of a nigger and teach em to find the nigger it belongs to, then a rag of his clothes, and so on. They always careful to tree the nigger, and teach the dog to wait and bark under the tree till they come up and give him his meat."

"Like training a dog to catch a raccoon," Josh said.

"No different," said Sam in a dry tone, "cept catching niggers pays better. You take Bill Gambel now. He get $5 a day for trailing a runaway with his pack of hounds, and $15 when he catch one. If the hunt take him more 'n ten miles from the starting place, he get another $10.

"Course, that's if no track is pointed out to him. If the slaveowner can start him on a track, then

Gambel's price is $25 outright for catching the slave. He brag his dogs can take the trail twelve hours after a nigger go by and catch him easy."

Sam gave three or four short, sharp puffs on his pipe, the white smoke jetting up over his dark face, then for a long interval just let the cob dangle from his mouth. It looked almost like an extension of the scar that ran down his face.

"Those dogs," he said, "they scared me sick, they were yelling so close by. I was too tired to run much more. I circled round and doubled on my tracks to mix up the hounds. Then I climbed a good tall tree. Soon I saw the pine knot of the overseer burning through the woods. The dogs were getting closer and closer. They smelled the tree I was in. Then they ran up and began barking around it. The overseer, he yelled to me to come down, but course I wouldn't. So he started up after me, and when he got close enough, he hit me over the head with a club. I lost my hold and tumbled down. When I hit the ground, the overseer let the hounds tear me a spell. They bit me here and there," he said, touching his breast and an arm, "and one of em did this." He drew his finger down the scar.

"They tied me on a horse and carried me home. Put me in the smokehouse every night, chained to a big log. Worked me all day in the fields, of course. Old Cabell see to that.

"Kept me there six weeks. Figured that any fool nigger would forget his troubles in that time. Then they let me go back to that empty cabin. Next time, I say to myself, next time I be a lot wiser."

Sam waited his time, acting as though he had forgotten his family. He found out from the house servants who the trader was who had taken Easter and the children away. With the help of the coachman, who wanted to pay off a grudge on Cabell, he found the trader operated out of Maysville, a town about forty miles off. That was where his family must have been sold. He had never been there and had to have the coachman explain which direction to head. The coachman forged a pass for Sam that said he was allowed to hire out his time in Maysville, and one night a month later, with food he had stowed away, he took to the woods again.

This time he ran with a pine brush tied behind him to drag his scent away. When he reached a lane running between two rail fences, he leaped up and walked on top for a long way. He waded streams and even rivers, often going out of his way to avoid leaving tracks.

When light broke he hid and, traveling only by

dark, reached the biggest river he had ever seen. It curved around one side of a town, and he knew this must be Maysville. He was sure Cabell was advertising him as a runaway, but he had shaved off his beard, and with a pass in his pocket and so many slaves walking the streets, going about their masters' business, he felt he could take the risk.

He struck up a conversation with a black and discovered the big river was the Ohio—and that on the other side of it was the free state of Ohio. He located Edward Stone's slavepen and, after patient efforts to make friends, won the confidence of a young slave who worked for the trader. He learned Easter had been bought as a house servant by a doctor living right in Maysville.

But their two children had been taken by another trader—he couldn't find out which—to be sold in New Orleans.

The next morning Sam lingered outside the doctor's home until he saw Easter leave for market. He followed her until it was safe to stop her.

"She begin to cry soon as she see me. I feel the same, but it too risky to let go. I put my hand over my mouth and motion her to keep walking. I catch up and we go side by side to an alley where no one see us. Then . . ." He paused and turned his face away.

"Well," he went on, "we find ways to meet. Each time we run over the same thing—what chance we have to find our children? Easter never want to give up. No more do I. But what we able to do? How we find our babies? Where?"

His voice trailed off. He reached for his clothing, now dry by the fire, and began to put it on. "It's no use, I tell Easter. I tell her ten times, a hundred times, till we both believe it. Then we ready to fix a way to get free ourselves.

"I study the river and how best we get over it. Careful all the time—talking to slaves or free blacks—careful I don't give away what we up to. There's patrollers watching the river where the crossings are. They keep an eye out for runaways on the boats, too. Folks get caught before they start. Or, they be taken on the river, and some even on this here side. You stay too long close by, and they kidnap you right back. Yet there be some get by them."

"But it's so close," said Josh. "I mean freedom. There's slavery on the Kentucky side, and here, just a swim across, is freedom. How come many more don't cross over?"

"That easy to ask," Sam said, "easy when you never been a slave. Hardly one of us but lays plans, year after year, to break free. But you give them up. You wake in the night thinking of a thousand things they put in your way. Every white man's hand raised against you. Your master, your overseer, they watching you, the patrollers watching you, the hounds hot for your track. And what you know about where to run? We not allowed more than a mile or two from the plantation. Most of us can't read nor write. We don't know how far free soil is, we don't know where river or forest or swamp may be that can hide us. Maybe if we lucky we learn about how the North Star points the way to freedom."

Josh could say nothing. He felt stupid.

"Bad off as you been," Sam said, "who knows if worse don't wait you?"

"Yet," Josh said, "you still tried to escape."

Sam laughed. "You scare yourself most into hell," he said, "but you living in hell now, so what be the difference?"

On a damp spring night they made their try. Sam had picked out a light boat that he had seen tied up to the shore on the side of town near where Easter lived. She went to bed as usual that night, but lay down in her clothes. Toward three in the morning she rose and slipped through the dark lanes till she reached their meeting place. They hid until the patrol passed, then crawled down to the bank, cut the rope and eased the boat into the water.

"Easter, she look scared, the way I feel inside. Only I try not to let her see how shaky I be. I have her get down on the bottom because every second I expect a patroller shoot at us.

"The current so strong, it hard to swing the boat where I want it to go. Can't see much of anything and the fog rolling in make it worse. But I can feel Easter's eyes on me. Don't dare hardly whisper. It feel like hours dragging by, rowing blind in the dark and worrying."

A faint rhythmic noise he had almost been unaware of began now to beat insistently in his ears. "I wonder, what's that? But I too busy trying to make that boat move to bother about anything else. Suddenly that sound—big now—seem like it hammering at my head. I see Easter jump up crazy-like. She point over my head and her mouth wide open screaming. I never forget how she look. A grinding noise cuts off her scream, the boat splinter all to pieces, we pitched over into the water. A steamboat come across our path and hit us. We so small and that boat so big and the night so dark no one see us. Can't swim, me nor Easter. I try to stay up, thrashing around, yelling for Easter. But no one hear me. The big boat's engines are too loud. I near wore out when a log come drifting close and I grab onto it. I keep calling out, 'Easter, Easter, Easter'—but no one answer. The night so fogged over I can't see a thing. Then I know it were no use.

"The current been carrying me farther and farther away all this time. I didn't know where it taking me. All stiff and aching from the cold. Can't hold on much longer. Then my log, it scrape against some rocks, shiver and stop. I just barely see I'm on some shore. I let go of the log, pull myself out of the river. Almost as soon as I lay myself down, I dead to the world."

When the sun rose an hour later, a patrol found him sleeping on the shore. He was still in Kentucky.

6

Remember Them That Are in Bonds

Josh lay awake while Sam slept. Fear soured his belly. Could that man on horseback have seen Sam on the raft? And gone for help? What if Sam were caught and blamed him? It must be a serious crime in a slave state to help a black get away. They could send him to prison, maybe even kill him. Sam stirred, restless on the hard ground. Josh saw a muscle in his cheek twitch and jump. He wondered what a man dreamed of who had gone through what Sam had.

When the patrollers found Sam on the shore, they had taken him back to his master. The overseer had lashed him till his skin came off in tatters, then kept him chained in the smokehouse every night. He'd been little use to the Cabells after that. Everything on the farm reminded him of Easter and his children. He sank into a bottomless misery. Finally the Cabells hired him out to a logger. For a year he had been cutting timber near the river. How he got through each day he didn't know. Endless hours with grief as solid as a stone in his chest, except when sleep brought a merciful forgetting. He had not even tried to plan another escape. Then, when he saw Josh's raft drifting by close to shore, it was as though the thick crust which shut out life had suddenly cracked open. He was ready to move.

Now Sam wanted to push on north, he said. He was worried about Cabell's agents hunting him down. Josh had found himself arguing against it. "Better work a while," he said, "and earn some money. You can get hired on as a woodcutter at my camp. The logger's short of hands. It's way back in the woods. No one ever comes near us. Then you'll be in better shape to strike out for Canada." Before he fell asleep, Sam had finally agreed. Josh thought it was because he was so uncertain about life on this side of the river. He needed time to learn, to feel more sure of himself.

There were still a few hours of dark to go when Josh woke him. They pushed the raft off shore and poled out into the current. They moved downstream; Sam lay concealed until they were miles past Maysville. They delivered the load. Two days later, they walked into the logging camp and headed for the boss logger's tent.

Josh suddenly had a feeling he'd better go in alone. Sam sat down on a wheelbarrow outside. After reporting on the delivery of the lumber—leaving Sam's part out—Josh said, "I've got a friend with me. Thought you'd want to take him on. He's a good man with an ax."

Mr. Dickey grinned. "If he's no bigger 'n you, Josh, I'll have to keep him to whittlin tent pegs."

"You got no complaint, Mr. Dickey. I more 'n keep up my end of it."

"That you do, boy. I'm only fooling. Where's your man?"

Josh nodded toward the tent opening. Dickey heaved himself up, waddled to the flap, and stuck his head out. He whirled around with astonishing speed for so heavy a man and, jerking a stiff arm back of him, he said, slowly and emphatically, "That—is—a—nigger."

"It is?"

"Sure as I am a white man, boy, that is a black man."

"Mr. Dickey, that is not news, not to me or to Sam."

"Then what you trying to be smart about?"

"Nothing, Mr. Dickey. Sam wants a job. You need woodcutters. That's all."

"That ain't all, boy. I done told you he's a nigger."

"Mr. Dickey, I knew he was black before you did. The thing is, he knows how to use an ax. Better than me. And you think I'm pretty good."

"That ain't the point. I'm from Virginia. Came all the way out here to get away from niggers."

"Mr. Dickey, I'm not asking you to live with Sam. Just to let him work for you."

"No lazy, good-for-nothin nigger's gonna work for me."

Josh was fighting to keep his voice calm. "I don't know what other black people you met up with, but I do know Sam. He can cut timber. He needs a job. He don't want to sit and jaw with you. He wants work, that's all."

"Never heard tell of a nigger like that! None of em want to work. And can't do nothin, either. Takes a white man to show em how and make em do it."

"All right," Josh said, "I can cut a day's timber, and you damn well know it. We need another man on our crew. Suppose you put Sam in my charge. He puts out what you expect of everyone else, or him and me both get fired. What have you got to lose?"

Mr. Dickey plumped himself down in his chair, turning his back on Josh. Josh stood there waiting. Then the fat man turned his head and said, "I take him on, he gets half what the other men get."

Half! Josh was furious. But what choice did Sam have? He ought to ask him would he accept it. But if he let this moment go by, maybe Dickey would change his mind and say no flat out. Besides, half pay was better than no pay. And Sam had done plenty of labor for no pay.

"All right, Mr. Dickey. He'll take it."

Dickey smiled. "Start him tomorrow, on your crew, and he better be good! Or it'll be your ass as well as his."

Josh came out of the tent expecting to find Sam angry. He knew he must have heard everything, sitting right outside the open flap. But Sam only laughed. "No use gettin mad," he said. "Old Dickey's a sly one. He know which end is up. Minds me of white trash back home. They like to see a nigger dead if they think he have more 'n they have."

There were two other whites in their crew, Scoles and Herrick, New England men. They were surprised to see a black man taken on. But if Dickey wanted it, they weren't going to say anything. None of the cutters stayed on the job long anyhow. They hired out for a season and then would be gone. Josh noticed Sam never took off his shirt in front of the others, and wondered why. Then he realized it was because Sam's back was crisscrossed with scars from whippings. If the men saw it, they would know he was a runaway slave.

One day, finding himself alone in the tent with Josh, Herrick said, "How come you and Sam such friends?"

"Why not? You and Scoles, you're friends too."

Herrick snorted. "That ain't what I'm saying. He's a nigger."

"Why's that bother you?"

"Well it don't really. But it don't seem right."

"That he's black?"

"Not that! Only you don't see a white man and a black man the way you two are."

"Maybe you would if you looked."

"Down here? And you been here this long already? Not even back home!"

He was right about that. Josh was silent.

Then Herrick said, "You an abolitionist?"

"What's that, Herrick?"

"You know as well as me. The people who say niggers are as good as whites."

"I thought they were people who believe slavery's wrong. And want to see it ended. *Abolished*—that's the word."

"Well, whatever it is, be you one of them?"

"Now I hadn't thought of that. Perhaps I am!" And he laughed.

Herrick, looking disgusted, went out of the tent.

Dickey had no complaints to make. Sam did his job, and the men let him alone. It was work and eat and sleep, with nothing else to do and no place to go.

Soon after heavy rains began, Josh came down with a bad cold. There was no chance to rest, and he couldn't seem to shake it. One day when they came back from cutting, Josh felt much worse; he was shivering all over. Sam tried to get him to quit but he wouldn't. The next day as they were hiking back to the camp they had to wade a river swollen from the rains. Trying to get up the steep bank on the far side, Josh slipped and dropped his ax. Before Sam could stop him he ducked for it several times. Just as he came up with it the ague took him. Soaked through to the skin he began shaking and puking till blood poured from his mouth. Sam lifted him onto his back and carried him to the camp a mile beyond.

There were no doctors near. Sam took over, letting Josh's blood and giving him plenty of barks and wine to break his fever. Josh slept for hours every day while Sam and the crew were out in the woods, then just after supper dozed off for the night. In two weeks he was well enough to take walks to build up his strength. One afternoon he got far enough from camp to find Sam cutting timber. Sam put down his ax, and they rested together on a log.

"Whyn't you go back to preaching, Josh? Not be so rough on you. This work in the woods may be too much."

Josh looked up at the sky. Above the tall pines he saw a flock of wild pigeons wheel past. In the topmost branches the wind was sighing.

"Never meant to stick here, Sam," he said. "But I like the woods. Used to walk in them alone all the time, back home. Makes me think of the stories the old folks tell about the woods—Indian wars, ghosts, witches. Scared me when I was little. But then the woods made me feel something else. Everything around me—the trees, the winds, the darkness, the sky, the moon and stars—I felt it was all the work of some power I couldn't see or even imagine. God, I guess. He seemed nearer to me then than He did in the Bible I was brought up on or the church we went to."

Sam sat silent. His palms were twirling the handle of the ax. "You still believe in Him?"

"In a different way from when I was a child."

"That religion your church preach—it don't mean much to me. Went to meeting every Sunday, regular, Easter and me, but we sure didn't feel the spirit there."

"Nor did I, Sam. Preacher Holman back home in Pike—I told you about him—he gave nobody faith. But you take Jacob Axley, there's a true man of God."

"I ain't talking about preachers. Talking about your religion. Now you tell me, if God love people, He want justice for them, don't He? And you preachers say He work through the church. All right— then what the church done about slavery?"

From his tone, it was plain Sam had an answer. He wants to know if I do, thought Josh.

"Well," Josh said, "I can speak only for my church, the Methodists. You can't find another church—except maybe the Quakers—that's set so strongly against it."

"Oh, that so?"

"Didn't John Wesley himself call it 'the sum of all villainies'?"

"If you tell me so, I suppose he did. But what your church *do* about it?"

"Why, fifty years ago, it said slavery was against the laws of God, man and nature, and it said Methodists who held slaves or traded in them should be punished."

"Good," said Sam. "And in those fifty years now, how many members been cast out?"

Josh fell silent. Sam knew the number as well as he. None.

"Tell me," Sam said. "What good it do—you, Axley, anyone—you preach up a storm at all those meetings, you get people flopping on their knees, praising God to the skies, promising to do good, and you do nothing about slavery? What do I care if a man get drunk of a Saturday night? Or he smoke a cob or chaw tobacco? Do the Devil take over the world if a boy and girl bed down together?"

"Sam, I preached so men and women would lead better lives."

Sam spat on the blade of his ax and tested the edge with his thumb. "And out of all that hollerin and moanin come what? Trimmed beards? Clean aprons? Promises to be good till next Saturday night?"

"The church can't do everything, Sam."

"But something! Something sides all that yammerin and promisin! Is they less slaves now than when you was born—or more? Tell me!"

Josh was shaken by Sam's rage. He'd lived with a man for months, only to find how little he knew of him. Oh, the outside facts, the events, these he knew from Sam's own telling. But at best, was it anything more than life at secondhand? Suddenly he felt a stranger to Sam.

Within the week Sam was gone. When he said good-bye to Josh, there was not a trace in his manner of the rage that had boiled over in the woods. He had taken his pay and was heading north. "Any-body ask about me," he told Josh, "you seen nothing."

He didn't have to say that, Josh thought. Would he have given Sam away? Didn't he help him escape? But there was a small doubt in his mind. If Sam had asked him for help under different circumstances, when there was more of a chance to make up his mind, what would he have done?

The next time Josh rafted logs on the river he kept close watch on the southern shore. He saw nothing unusual. *Remember them that are in bonds, as bound with them.* The words echoed in Josh's head. Words mouthed in countless pulpits. Remember. Remember.

Two weeks passed, and then one day he took a

ferry across the Ohio to set foot for the first time on slave territory. He had saved much of his pay. And he could work. He could even preach and pass the hat, if it came to that.

7

Kentucky Bluegrass

The ferry set Josh down in Maysville. He took a room in a boardinghouse and started looking around. Bluegrass country. The brick mansions of the planters, sitting way back from the road, in groves of great trees. He saw their elegant carriages sweeping out of the long driveways, black coachmen at the reins.

Within a day or two people knew there was a stranger in town. They were polite to him, but inquisitive. Who might he be? Where from? And what might he be doing here? The first time, he didn't know what to answer. What *was* he doing here? "I'm a preacher," he had blurted out, "Methodist." That helped. Kentucky was Methodist country. "Thinking maybe I'll settle down here."

At the general store one morning he met the Reverend Billy Shaw, a short, lean man, sallow of skin, with a squinting eye and a high-pitched, penetrating voice. "This young man's looking for a place to stay," said the storekeeper, introducing them. "And he's a Methodist preacher too."

"Methodist preacher, is it? Well, so 'm I, so 'm I. Though I don't do much preaching these days. Now and then to the niggers, that's all. Niggers 'n mules, that's what white folks make their living on," he said with a laugh. "The preaching ain't much any more. Not for me, it ain't."

A few days later when they met again in the store, Shaw asked Josh to come and spend a while at his farm. Plenty of room, he said, "And you can take your time deciding what to do next." If only I liked this man, Josh thought; it would be easier.

He picked up his few things at the boardinghouse, and they rode out to Shaw's place in his wagon. A ramshackle frame building. Nothing like those brick mansions. Everything about it was slovenly. Hogs, hounds and black and white children playing outside. Inside, few of the comforts a Northern farmer took for granted.

Shaw raised corn, oats, hay and fruits, with four families of slaves to do the work. Their cabins out back were flimsy one-room huts with earthen floors and small openings in the sides for windows. The chimneys were made of sticks and mud, the doors of rough boards. Shaw gave them no furniture or household utensils. They slept on cornhusk mattresses.

Shaw was a sloppy farmer. Josh could see that quickly. Didn't know much about it and hadn't the ambition to learn. He let the blacks do their work the way it had always been done, good or bad. He wasn't interested in finding out if there was a better way. Once Josh made a suggestion, and Shaw laughed it off. "Don't make no matter of difference," he said. "Just as easy to do it this way." No wonder he seemed to be in debt all the time, borrowing so he could keep his head above water. Or hiring out a slave or two.

Josh soon found out that what kept Shaw's place going was Aunt Annie and her husband Bob. With their four children, one a little baby, they lived in one of the cabins. Annie was a long, lean woman with copper skin and straight black hair. Part Indian, back somewhere. She could do anything. She cooked, washed, ironed, spun, sewed, nursed and worked in the fields. "Good a field hand as she is a cook," Shaw bragged to Josh. "Annie has her faults, but she can outwork any nigger in the county. I'd bet my life on that."

What faults? Josh got a clue one day when he overheard Annie singing:

We raise de wheat,
Dey gib us de corn;
We bake de bread,
Dey gib us de crus;
We sif de meal,
Dey gib us de skin,
And dat's de way
Dey take us in.
We skim de pot,
Dey gib us de liquor,
And say dat's good enough for de nigger.
   Walk over! Walk over!
   Tom butter and de fat;
Poor nigger you can't get over dat;
   Walk over!

When she was willing to work, she was Shaw's "good" slave. But if she didn't feel like doing something, no one could make her do it. At least Shaw couldn't, or didn't even try. For when Annie fussed, they could hear her almost down to Maysville. Shaw tried to overlook it. Josh thought it was because he was scared.

One day while Annie was bustling about Shaw's

house, cleaning, Josh heard her mutter angrily, "No-suh, no man can whip me no more!" Like little explosions from some running battle going on inside her.

Sitting within earshot of the kitchen, Josh heard her telling her oldest daughter, "I'll kill you, gal, if you don't stand up for yourself." The child, she was only about nine, murmured something in reply, and then Annie said angrily, "Fight, and if you can't fight, kick, and if you can't kick, then bite!"

He heard her argue with her husband, too. Bob usually subsided into silence quickly. And then she'd say, "Bob, I don't want no sorry nigger round me. I can't tolerate you if you ain't got no backbone."

Bob was plowman, gardener, yardman, black-smith, carpenter, keysmith—whatever Shaw needed. Yet he found time somehow to take care of the little garden near their cabin, and he also had chickens. Shaw let him make a little money on the side by selling to Brown's hotel in town. Brown didn't know it, but sometimes he was buying Shaw's own stuff, not Bob's.

Josh didn't talk much to the slaves on the place. Shaw would have wondered why, if he had tried. Nor would Josh have gotten very far anyway; why should the slaves trust him? He just kept his eyes and ears open. He found out that Shaw had had children by one of the slaves on the farm. Mrs. Shaw, a sickly woman in spite of her fat, acted as if she didn't know it, even though anyone could see who the father was. A year back, when his debts got too pressing, Shaw had sold two of his own slave children.

Josh had been on the farm a couple of weeks when Shaw asked him if he'd like to come hear him preach to the blacks on the next Sunday. He surely would. The whites from all the farms around attended morning service. Every fourth Sunday, in the afternoon, the slaves were allowed to go to the same church. It had long wooden benches, and a table and chair in the center for the preacher. Shaw brought an old brown leather-backed Bible. He set it in the middle of the table but never looked at it. A few whites joined Josh as he took a seat in the back row. They were patrollers, they told him. The services started with a hymn, "Amazing Grace."

Then the preacher began his sermon. First he told how God in His wisdom had provided a place for everyone:

"That's why some be masters and mistresses, some merchants and lawyers, and some," he said, "God made servants and slaves. Why? To help your masters and mistresses who provide for you. God has His own good reason why He send each one of us into this world. So we all obliged, yes, every last one of us, to do the business He set us. And all you good folk He made slaves. Don't think while you do your business, honestly and peacefully, and live like poor Christians ought to live, that you not serving God in *your* place just as much as the President, sitting way up there in Washington in the White House!

"You there, Simon! You want to have your soul saved by Jesus? And you, Emmy, you want to escape hell and get into heaven? Then you got to do what God wants—to serve *Him!* That be the way to take care of your soul!"

The preacher's voice lowered. He spoke slowly, confiding a great and precious secret:

"And how can you do that? By doing your service for your master and mistress as—if—you—did—it—for—God—Himself!"

He shook his head sorrowfully.

"You poor, poor folk! You don't think, when you idle, and you neglect your master's business, and you steal and waste, and you act sassy, and you tell lies, and you stubborn, and you don't do the work set out for you without stripes—that the faults you guilty of toward *you* master and mistress are faults done *against God Himself!*

"*He* has set your master and mistress over you

in His own place. And *He* expect you do for them just what you would do for *Him* . . .

"You know," he said, "your master and mistress—they be *nothing but God's overseers.* And if you mean to them, God Himself will punish you for it in hell!"

He had worked himself up till he was red in the face and sweating. He paused now, mopping his face, then spoke quietly:

"That why you got to be obedient to your master and please him well, in all things. Remember, it be God who wants this from you, and if you not afraid of suffering for it in *this* world [and here he looked straight at Annie], you will not escape the vengeance of God Almighty in the *next* world!"

And giving his old leather Bible a mighty wallop that boomed to the rafters, Shaw sat down.

As though a barrier had suddenly been dropped, the black worshippers tore into a hymn that rocked the old walls: "Ride on, King Jesus, no man can hinder Thee."

Next to Josh, a patroller who had dozed through the sermon stirred uneasily and grumbled, "They better stop, or I'll show em can they be hindered."

"Like my preaching?" Shaw said, riding back to the farm.

"Never heard anything like it," Josh replied.

"You hear big preachers up North, I bet!"

"But their style doesn't come near miles of yours."

Shaw sighed. "Maybe it be a mistake for me, farming. Preaching's a lot easier on a man. How about you trying it next time?"

"Oh, no!" Josh said. "Wouldn't know how to preach to black folks the way you do. They wouldn't pay me any mind."

8

School for Abolitionists

A confused shouting broke out below in the kitchen. Josh could hear pots banging and then a crash as though a chair had been hurled against a wall. He raced down the stairs, and as he reached the entryway Mrs. Shaw came running out with Annie hot on her heels. In the yard Annie caught up and started ripping off Mrs. Shaw's clothing. She pulled and twisted and tore her mistress half-naked before Josh could get to them.

"What are you doing, Annie, what are you doing?" he hollered, begging her to stop. He knew the terrible punishment laid on slaves for striking their masters.

"I'll kill her. I'll kill her dead if she ever hits me again!" Annie kept yelling.

At last he succeeded in wrenching the woman free of Annie's grip. Mrs. Shaw went sobbing into the house, clutching her clothes about her, trembling with fear and anger.

Annie slumped to the ground, sitting with her back against the fence. She seemed suddenly drained of energy. Her eyes were closed. He squatted beside her.

"What started all this, Annie?"

Her eyes still closed, she said, "Missus hit me with a stick. I hit her back."

"But why'd she hit you? Did you do something?"

She opened one eye and squinted up at him. "White boy," she said, "that none of your business." The eye closed.

When Shaw came back that afternoon and heard what had happened he said, "Annie's got to be whipped, or she won't know she's a nigger." But he'd have her whipped by the law. He did not relish trying to do it himself.

The next morning two men came in at the gate, one with a long lash in his hand. Josh saw them arrive and ducked around the corner of the house to warn Annie, who was working in the back garden. To his surprise, she only looked contemptuously at him, dropped her hoe, and started running straight for where the men were. He watched her swoop down on them like a hawk on chickens. They were startled by her and didn't know what to do. They thought she was crazy. She grabbed one by his long beard and with her other hand seized the lash. She had the strength of a madman, and though they twisted and turned and tried to wrestle her to the ground, they couldn't break her hold.

Seeing that one of the men was trying to pull a gun from his belt, Josh started forward. He had taken only a few steps when Shaw came tearing up and grabbed the man's wrist. Annie caught sight of the gun.

"Shoot!" she yelled. "Shoot and blow my brains out!" But when Shaw ordered her back to the garden, she went.

That night Shaw went down to Annie's cabin and called her out. "Annie," he said, "we have to send you away. You won't be whipped; you'll only get yourself killed. We'll have to knock you down like a beef. And you no good to me that way."

"I'll go to hell or anyplace else," Annie said, "but I won't be whipped."

Shaw stood for a moment saying nothing. Then, "Annie, you can't take the children. Nor the baby, either. Aunt Rose will keep it with the others."

She looked at him, then turned and went inside.

"What are you going to do?" Josh asked Shaw that night.

"Hire em out," he said. "Annie and Bob both. He'll only mope around without her. That pair will bring me good money in Lexington."

"What about the children?"

"No problem. I can use the older ones right now and sell em when I need cash. The baby'll be a nuisance for a time. But she'll soon get big enough to more 'n pay her way."

"Why don't you let Annie take care of her, then?"

"Needs a lesson, that one. Seems like I can't get at her any other way. Ever see a nigger like that? No feelings at all!"

The morning they were to leave, Josh saw Annie moving around the place with her baby under her arm. She never put the child down. Not for a second. Shaw rode up to the cabin trailing an old mare for Annie and an old mule for Bob.

"Annie, I'm ready. Leave the baby with Aunt Rose," he said.

At this, Annie faced Shaw, took her baby by the feet, and swung her head downward. "I'll smash her brains out before I'll leave her," she said. Tears streamed down her face.

When they rode off, Shaw was in the rear, Bob in the middle, and Annie up front, the baby cradled in her arms.

All that day, whenever Josh passed by Annie's children, they were crying. By evening their eyes looked like coals of fire.

He slept badly that night. If only Annie had run away with her family. But it wasn't that easy . . . he'd learned that much from Sam. Perhaps she too had been waiting for the right word, the right moment. He should have found some means to help her. Instead, he had stood aside, watching. But Annie wouldn't trust him. Still, he should have tried. Nothing would have been made worse than it already was. He should have taken the chance; she might have said yes. But if she had, what would he have done? For a moment he wondered if he had simply been too scared.

He fell asleep at last. In the morning, he got up determined not to stay a day longer. He'd find someone who could show him how to do what he was thinking of. Levi Coffin—that was the man. His name was known all over these parts now. A Quaker storekeeper, he'd left his native North Carolina a dozen years ago because abolitionists were finding it impossible to survive at home. With his wife Kate he'd settled on the free side of the Ohio, where they had recruited many neighbors to help shelter fugitive slaves until they could be sent on to Canada.

Josh found the Coffins near Cincinnati and told

them about Sam and then about his stay on Shaw's farm in Kentucky. But when he revealed what he had in mind, Levi Coffin did not like it. Josh wanted to go into the South to take slaves out? No, said Levi, at no time or under any circumstances would he solicit or advise a slave to leave his master.

"But who is doing more to oppose slavery than you?" Josh said.

"That's not the point. It isn't my business to go down there and interfere with their laws or their slaves."

"The laws! You don't believe the master really owns the slave! He belongs to himself, the way you do! There's no justice in a law that treats Annie or Sam like cattle!"

"We don't quarrel with that," put in Kate. "But to venture into the South, that's plain reckless. I think it would do more harm than good."

"How could that be! Suppose just one slave is saved. How can that do any harm?"

"Look at it this way, Josh," said Levi. "You're burning to relieve the suffering of the slave. But how many could you possibly help to escape by your own efforts? A handful? Thousands of slaves run away on their own, without any whites helping them. Think, now. What effect would your actions have upon the whole mass of slaves? Their masters will simply bind them tighter in chains. We'll have more success in reaching the consciences of the slave-holders by an open and honorable course. We need young folks like you to abolitionize Ohio."

Josh stood up.

"Wait, Josh," Levi said. "The antislavery society is opening a school in New York to train agents. Why don't you go?"

"I don't want to be shut away in any school. I want to be where things are happening."

"What did you come see me for, then? I thought you felt the need of being prepared. It's only a month's training, Josh, and you'll be in the hands of the best. Theodore Weld will be running the school."

Weld! Josh had heard of him. From Jacob Axley, the first time. "A man of reckless righteousness," Jacob had said. "Saves all his hell-fire and damnation for the slaveholders." A one-man army of abolition, Weld would sweep into the upstate New York villages and night after night hold meetings to abolitionize them. Mobs had attacked him many times, but even when badly hurt, he would never quit.

"I thought you'd like that," said Levi. "Weld's made so many converts all by himself, the antislavery society has decided to multiply him many times over. The school is their way of doing it. They want seventy young men to come. When you finish, you'll be scattered all through the country districts of the North. This is the way to do it. It's building a *movement* that will change things. If we make enough converts to abolition, public opinion may be able to push Congress into changing the law some day, so slavery will be ended. Try it, Josh. If I recommend you, they'll take you."

So he went to New York and for twenty days was bombarded with facts and philosophy, most of it poured on by Weld. "He carries his conscience on his face," one student said of him. Weld was the master spirit, but William Lloyd Garrison and several other leaders were there too. Josh was startled to find how quiet and mild-mannered was the dread Boston editor whose words in his newspaper *The Liberator* had so enraged the slaveholders.

The trainees lived close together during the schooling period. Like himself, the others were young, some still students in college, some fledgling preachers. On their own, they asked the Grimké sisters, Sara and Angelina, to join them. The daughters of South Carolina slaveholders, they took an equal part with the men in discussions, speaking freely whenever they liked. Except for Josh's limited view of Kentucky, theirs and Weld's were the only firsthand accounts of slavery the students heard.

For eight hours on end, day after day, Josh listened to lectures. And half the night they stayed up talking about the same things—the history and nature of slavery, colonization, gradual versus immediate emancipation, the Bible argument against slavery, the condition of free blacks, the changes they hoped the freeing of the slaves would make in American life.

Every objection to the cause was taken up, discussed and answered. Weld saw to it that they learned how to handle audiences from veterans who had been long in the field. One night one of New York's black abolitionist preachers talked to them. On another night, Amos Dresser, a young theological student from Massachusetts, told them of his recent ordeal in Nashville. He had gone to Tennessee to sell Bibles. Found with an antislavery newspaper in his trunk, he was given twenty lashes on his bare back in the town square, then run out of town.

Josh wondered whether Amos had gone into the South really to sell Bibles. One night he cornered Dresser.

"Amos, you said you were selling Bibles down there?"

"I was trying to, Josh."

"But more?"

"What are you getting at?"

"I thought maybe, well, you had that abolitionist paper they found in your trunk?"

"I did. I never denied it was mine."

"I was thinking perhaps you were distributing abolitionist literature . . . or helping slaves to run off."

"Why do you say that? Are you thinking of it yourself?"

"You haven't answered me, Amos."

"I'm not trying to avoid the question. The truth is, I don't know. I did not help any slaves. I might have—but then there wasn't time. They got suspicious of me, found that paper, and that was the end. If I'd been able to stay, it could have come out a different story. I just don't know what I would have done."

"Well, what about now?"

"It isn't what we're here for, Josh. The society is training us to spread the abolition idea in the North. Maybe we'll build enough of a following so some day abolitionists will even run for office—I know Garrison's against that, but some say that's bound to come."

"Most everyone here seems to think the moral appeal is everything. Touch the conscience of men and women, and they will change."

"I believe in that, too, Josh. But what happened to me in Nashville—the hate, the cruelty, so many people blind to fact, deaf to reason, hardened to feeling—it shook me. And it isn't just the Southerners. Not one person of prominence in my own state made any public complaint about my flogging. You think the Southerners would respond that way if one of theirs was flogged in Massachusetts?"

By the end of Weld's teaching, Josh was flaming hot.

When it came time to leave, he thought about stopping in Pike. It was so long since he had seen his mother and father. He had written, but just enough to let them know he was all right. They knew he had been logging in Ohio. If he saw them now, they'd want to know what he meant to do. Should he tell them? He didn't want them to try to stop him. And he knew they would. Besides, the longer he stayed away, the harder it was to think of finding any way to talk to his father again. Am I getting to be like him? he wondered.

He wrote to his mother:

Dear Ma,

How are you? I hope you've been well and everything on the farm is going all right. Nothing much to tell you about me. My work keeps me outdoors and healthy—though I haven't grown an inch. If you see Jacob, tell him I'm all right. And say hello to Pa.

Love,
Josh

He read the letter over, sealed it, and was about to mail it. Then he stuck it in his pocket. Better to send it when he'd be back in Ohio.

9

Is This God's House?

In parts of Ohio Weld had already broken the sod for abolition. Scattered through the towns and villages were dozens of antislavery societies. Josh knew he had friends to count on; he soon discovered there were many enemies too.

It began in Slotesville, where he tried a tactic Weld had taught him. He went to the Methodist church on a Sunday morning, taking a seat in a pew near the middle. He met curious glances with a smile. During the long prayer the whole congregation rose, but when they sat down again, he remained on his feet.

"I wish to speak a few words in behalf of millions of our countrymen kidnapped and enslaved," he said in a low voice, holding tightly to the pew in front of him. Everyone's face turned to him, startled. The minister leaned over the pulpit, his hand outstretched as if to stop him.

"Slavery is branded as a sin against God and a crime against man almost everywhere," he went on. "Every man has a right to his own body, to the fruits of his labor, to the protection of law. It is piracy by our laws to buy or steal a native African and subject him to servitude.

"Surely the sin is as great to enslave an American. Every American citizen who holds a human being in bondage is a manstealer. Did we not learn it long ago? 'And he that stealeth a man, and selleth him, or if he be found in his hand, he shall surely be put to death.'

"I look at the Book of Discipline that every Methodist house contains, and find in it that no Methodist who desires salvation can take part in the 'buying and selling of men, women and children with an intention to enslave them.'

"Yet I know—you all know it—that Methodist members and ministers still hold tens of thousands of slaves. They hold them as goods and chattels, they rob them of the right to marry. No house of prostitution in New York is guilty of such an abomination. For there the victims can escape, but in our Southern churches they are held, compelled by both religion and government, to stay and endure their slavery.

"Can any Christian who tolerates this be excused? Is he free of sin and shame?

"Listen to this," he said and took out of his pocket an advertisement. "This is a clipping from the Charleston, South Carolina, *Courier*. It says:

FIELD NEGROES BY THOMAS GADSDEN. ON TUESDAY, THE 17TH INSTANT, WILL BE SOLD AT THE NORTH OF THE EXCHANGE AT 10:00 A.M. A PRIME GANG OF TEN NEGROES, ACCUSTOMED TO THE CULTURE OF COTTON AND PROVISIONS—BELONGING TO THE INDEPENDENCE CHURCH, IN CHRIST CHURCH PARISH.

"What have we here but trade in slaves and souls of men *by the church itself!*

"And here, from another newspaper, I read you this item:

ON THE FIRST OF MONDAY OF FEBRUARY NEXT, WILL BE PUT UP AT PUBLIC AUCTION, BEFORE THE COURTHOUSE, THE FOLLOWING PROPERTY BELONGING TO THE ESTATE OF THE LATE REVEREND DR. FURMAN, VIZ.: A PLANTATION OR TRACT OF LAND, ON AND IN THE WATEREE SWAMP. A TRACT OF THE FIRST QUALITY OF FINE LAND, ON THE WATERS OF BLACK RIVER. A LOT OF LAND IN THE TOWN OF CAMDEN. A LIBRARY OF A MISCELLANEOUS CHARACTER, CHIEFLY THEOLOGI-

CAL. TWENTY-SEVEN NEGROES, SOME OF THEM
VERY PRIME. TWO MULES, ONE HORSE AND AN
OLD WAGON.

He looked up from the clipping. "Who does not know the words from the Declaration of Independence, 'All men are created equal'? Mr. Jefferson meant that all men, at creation, are equal. But Dr. Furman had another breed of men, seven and twenty of them, and two mules and one horse, or thirty in all, and all 'created equal.' And one old wagon— we must not forget—just as 'equal' as the rest. And the Independence Church in Christ Church parish, it had ten more."

The congregation was buzzing now. Who was this lunatic? What did he want of them? Voices rose louder, interrupting him.

"Wait a minute!" he called out. "Have you heard? Two mules, a horse, and an old wagon, and twenty-seven Negroes, 'some of them very prime.' Does any mortal man or woman understand the meaning of those words?"

From the pulpit the minister called out angrily, "You, sir! You, sir! We must not be disturbed in our worship!"

But Josh would not stop.

"Is there any remedy for the sin of slavery but

the immediate and unconditional emancipation of every slave? No slaveholder can be a Christian! We must not permit fellowship with slaveholders in our church!"

Now one of the church elders, a dignified, portly man, stalked across the aisle and, seizing Josh by the shoulders, shook him. "Quiet, boy!" he said. "You have no right to interrupt our worship!"

"Would you force me out of the church only for speaking? Is this God's house?" Josh asked, turning to the congregation. "Is it right to speak for the slave here? Right to wake up sleeping deacons and ministers? To ask them to lift their heel from the neck of my wife, brother, sister, mother? To cry robber in the ear of a church that buys, sells and enslaves God's own image? That sells Jesus Christ at auction and then declares it has not violated the Christian faith?"

He was shouting now, his voice trembling with anger. Several people were rising and hurrying out of the church. One woman leaped up and called out, "Stay! Hear the truth!" Hands tugged at his arms to pull him down into his seat. Suddenly two men came up at him from behind and dragged him down the aisle with savage fury. He did not resist, letting himself go limp, but they threw him down the steps when they reached the door.

Now the whole congregation was jamming the entrance, furiously arguing, some defending the sacredness of the church, others attacking the minister for permitting the violence. A few went over to him, where he stood brushing off his clothes and gingerly feeling his bruises.

"Are you hurt, son?" an old lady asked.

"No, ma'am. I don't think so."

"Thank God. You made trouble here, son. Now don't say you didn't mean to! You surely did—and it was past time somebody did! Will you be staying on a while?"

"I can't. I must get on to another meeting."

"Well, you come again, you hear? And by the time you do, I'll see you get a better welcoming!"

Josh was not the only one to meet violence. Sleeping in a Quaker's store one night, Marius Robinson was dragged out, carried ten miles off, stripped naked, beaten, tarred and feathered and dumped on the roadside at daybreak. At Middlebury, James Thome and John Alvord so riled the village with abolition lectures two nights running that on the third a mob broke into the meeting with a broadside of rotten eggs. Abolitionists in that place had always been driven out. This time it was different: enough villagers had come over to their side to kick out the mob.

At Harding some boys shoved a fierce-looking dog through the window as Josh was speaking. He went right on. The dog padded up and down the aisles, barked once or twice, lay down by the stove and was soon asleep, much to the audience's amusement. They were often egged, but Josh told himself good came of it. Abolitionists were hatched out of the public's anger at the violation to free speech. Mobs usually showed themselves to be great cowards. They seldom did more than threaten and throw stones or snowballs. That helped the cause by turning waverers to its support.

The first time Josh went out on a long swing it was the heart of winter. For three months he traveled by horseback, wagon and sleigh. Some places were open to his message, others coldly hostile. In Steubenville he came across a young abolitionist running classes for black children. "The school's flourishing," he told Josh, "but no white will speak to me." In Cincinnati, abolitionists were working among the blacks, organizing clubs, employment agencies, schools.

He stopped at the Coffins' for a night, the first time he'd seen them since returning from Weld's school.

"I see you lads are in the papers," Levi said, taking out a clipping. " 'A pestilent handful of fanatics plotting freedom for niggers'—that's what this editor says."

Kate laughed. "I guess Weld's a good teacher," she said.

In Licking County he ran into mild trouble. Only three of his ten lectures were interrupted. When he reached Granville, worse threatened. On trees everywhere he saw this placard:

ABOLITIONISTS!

A HIRED AGENT OF THESE FANATICS HAS GIVEN PUBLIC NOTICE THAT HE WILL ATTEMPT THIS EVENING TO ARRAY THE *North* AGAINST THE *South*—TO VIOLATE THE PRINCIPLES OF THE CONSTITUTION—AND TO PREACH A DOCTRINE WHICH WILL *revolutionize* AND *disunionize* THE COUNTRY—AND LEAD TO ALL THE *Blood Horrors of a Civil War.* CITIZENS OF GRANVILLE—LOVERS OF YOUR COUNTRY—*Will you permit this?*

Hall, warehouse, store—all in Granville were closed to him. But finally a minister volunteered his church. He was about half an hour into his lecture when military music began to drown out his voice. The door opened and in marched a three-piece band—big bass drum, little snare drum and a bugle.

The musicians marched up into the gallery, playing all the while, and sat there blasting away. He waited for them to tire, but the moment they paused, the bell in the belfry started tolling. His audience, a large one, sat patiently, waiting out the noisemakers. Then in came the head selectman, and the band broke off.

"I hear there is a riot here," he said, "but I see none." And turning to the peaceable citizens in the pews: "I direct you all to disperse!"

At this there was loud grumbling and a few jeers, but they rose and left, motioning Josh to follow. Outside, standing on the grass, they held their own meeting, formed an antislavery society and signed scores of members on the spot.

Not often did such a threatening beginning end so well. But usually if Josh came back night after night, the violence died away. The troublemakers tired faster than he did. And then he signed more recruits to immediate abolition. In each place the converts he made became a recruiting center for more converts as he moved on.

Always he gave people a chance to stand up and talk about slavery. To ask questions, voice feelings, describe experiences. What moved Josh most at such times was the sight of a Southerner rising to give testimony against slavery. Some of these were now

Ohioans, so it was perhaps easier for them to talk honestly about what they had left behind. But now and then there was a slaveholder on a visit to a relative or friend. And even such a man would sometimes be moved to rise and testify.

The long winter on the road wore Josh down. "Your voice is almost gone," Levi said to him one day. "You're not much use without it. Better stay with us and rest a while."

He was grateful for the chance to sit and do nothing. When April's thaw came, he started again, this time trying the southeastern belt of counties. They lay along the Ohio. He abolitionized from village to village, and found he couldn't tell what would come up next. In one place there was a strong feeling against slavery. People told him they had often gone across the river to Kentucky, had seen slavery, knew what it was, hated it. In the next place they said, "Stay away from here. We trade with the Kentucky folk. Don't want you messing around. Slavery's their business, not ours. Nor *yours*."

The next time he stopped at the Coffins', Levi sensed a change in him before he could say a word.

"You're going south again, Josh."

"Don't try to talk me out of it."

"I know it'd do no good."

"Levi, there's nothing wrong with what you're

all doing. But see what's happening! Down South they're burning *The Liberator*, they're passing laws to bar abolition literature from the mails, they're driving out their own people who dare say a word against slavery. How can they be reached?"

"Only by keeping at it, not by giving up."

"I know what you're doing has to be done, Levi. If we don't keep talking to people, organizing them, they'll never move against slavery. But it'll take so long!"

"You're still very young, Josh."

"Maybe so. But every day I get older, the slave gets a day older too."

"What are you going to do?"

"Think about people like Annie. She was ready to turn, ready to move. Now maybe I could do something—a word, a hand, money, I don't know what—anything to clear the way out."

"You know how I feel, Josh. I wouldn't send you south. But if you're going anyhow, maybe I can help cut down the risks."

First, they thought of what disguise would be best. Josh could go as a peddler, his pack filled with cheap goods slaves could afford and fancy goods for their mistresses. Other abolitionists had tried this, finding it opened doors to the big house and the slave quarters alike. But men as young as Josh didn't go into this trade. It wouldn't look right, and he wouldn't be comfortable in the part. No, better stick to what he was (or had been), a preacher. There were many circuit riders in the slave states, and he would be thoroughly at home. They agreed on a simple code for sending messages. Josh could warn Levi and Kate when to be on the watch for any fugitives he could send on to them.

A day before he was to leave, a Kentucky lawyer named Dennis Seals visited Coffin to ask if he could help arrange a slave rescue. Seals was concerned about the case of William Minnis, a young black he knew back in Jessamine County, about fifteen miles from Lexington. Minnis had been willed free upon his master's death. But he had been kept ignorant of the will, even by the executor of the estate and others sworn to inform such legatees of their rights. When the master died, his son and heir had sold William to the Lexington slave trader, Billy Pullum.

"I know him," Josh said. "Shaw introduced us one day at the general store in Maysville." Pullum had a face Josh would not forget easily. He was a slight man, about forty, with chestnut hair turning gray. His mouth looked like a knife wound. Seals said Pullum had taken Minnis to Little Rock, Arkansas. There a businessman named Brennan had bought him. "I've known William from childhood and am very fond of him," Seals said. "The law's the law. They cheated William of his freedom. I mean to see he gets it."

They sat around the kitchen table figuring out a rescue plan.

"But *who* will do it?" Seals asked. "I ought to take the risk myself, but it wouldn't do William any good. Too many people know me in Little Rock."

Kate suggested an abolitionist lawyer from Cincinnati or one of their neighbors who'd sheltered many fugitive slaves. For one reason or another, neither man was quite right. No one seemed to think of Josh. Not even himself, at first. But as they discussed the difficulties of a rescue, and the necessity of finding just the right man for it, he began to feel he was the best choice. People that far off wouldn't know him, and he was young enough not to be suspected by anyone.

When he spoke up, the others didn't take him seriously. When he persisted, Seals pointed out the great dangers in moving through hundreds of miles of slave territory. Many who had tried to aid slaves to escape had either lost their lives or rotted away in prison. But no matter what obstacles they raised, Josh wanted to go. And the next day—perhaps because no one else was there to do it—they agreed.

He set off, $200 in his pocket, put up by Seals. He knew no more than William's name, what he looked like and the name of his owner. Three days later he arrived in Little Rock and began a careful search that had to appear careless and indifferent.

He was wrong to think no one would notice him. The whites suspected any stranger until he proved he was no enemy of slavery. The slaves suspected any white. He might be a slave speculator looking for bargains. So he was held at arm's length by the one, and fenced with very ingeniously by the other.

It took him four weeks to learn what he had to know. Mr. Brennan, it appeared, was often away on business, traveling by river from town to town. William had been hired out as a hotel porter. He worked and lived in the Little Rock House.

Josh took a room at that hotel and contrived a way to see William alone. He called for a servant to carry his carpetbag to the boat.

"Master, that not my work," the slave said. "That William's work. He do that work." And he called across the lobby, "William! See here! This gentleman wants you!"

Up came a well-built lad about Josh's size, and just a few years younger. His skin's almost as light as mine, Josh thought. That'll help. The boy took

Josh's bag, and they walked out into the street. Josh was silent for a little way before venturing to ask, "What's your name?"

"William Minnis, sir."

No mistake, then.

"How long have you been in this city?"

"Well, master, just about a year ago I left Lexington. I was bought by the trader Mr. Pullum, and he fetch me here and sell me. I belong to Mr. Brennan. He hire me out here at the hotel."

So Josh had the whole story.

"Did your master live in Jessamine County?"

"Yes, sir."

"He died, and his son sold you, eh?"

"Yes, sir. Did you know him?"

"Yes. William, did you know Dennis Seals?"

"Yes, sir."

"Did you know that your master willed you free before he died? And your young master sold you, knowing all about it?"

"No sir! I did not! I did not! I did not!" William was stunned. He stopped short and dropped Josh's bag.

Quietly Josh said, "Go back with my bag, William. I won't take the boat. Come to my room tonight as early as you can."

In the weeks he had been in Little Rock, Josh

had figured out how to make the escape once William was found. He had made friends with a Creole barber and a young Massachusetts schoolmistress, who also painted portraits. He confided in both as soon as he found they were deeply opposed to slavery.

That night Minnis met him in his room. Josh needed to know of some white man William could be made to look very much like—with wig, beard, mustache, clothing. In a few minutes, William had the answer—a young man from up the river, Mr. Young, a casual acquaintance of Mr. Brennan's. Physically they were similar. The barber would do up William so that he could pass for Mr. Young— a wig of long black hair, and whiskers and mustache in the Southern style. The Yankee artist would lighten his complexion. They would take the boat that left at twilight for the trip down the Arkansas to the Mississippi, then up that river to where it met the Ohio, which would carry them to Cincinnati. But since Mr. Brennan often took the same boat as far as the Mississippi on his way to Vicksburg, master and slave might meet on board. "In case that happens," Josh said, "Mr. Minnis must be ready to play Mr. Young."

They worked out every detail. At first William was very nervous. Josh worried how William would carry off the masquerade until he realized this was all as new to himself. He would wake at three in the morning, sweating over all the things that could go wrong. The days seemed to ooze by as he waited for the safest moment. Meanwhile he and William avoided being seen together.

Josh packed his bag at noon each day. Finally all seemed right. They took the risk of a dress rehearsal the night before the boat was to leave. The four of them met in the room behind the barber's shop. By now, William could play a fine Southern cavalier. Raised as a house servant from childhood, his speech wasn't much different from his master's.

The next day, a half hour before sailing time, William left the hotel on some excuse and was swiftly made up and costumed in the barber's back room. Josh stayed to settle his bill, then struck out for the wharf. Before he reached it, "Mr. Young" joined him, casually swinging a gold-headed cane. In a few minutes they were aboard and in the lounge. There was nothing any longer to be gained by close association, so they drifted apart to mingle with the other passengers.

An hour later William came up to Josh at the rail and, standing beside him for a moment, whispered, "Mr. Brennan's on the boat."

Not looking at him, Josh said calmly, "Put on airs."

William cleared his throat and walked away.

Very soon, strolling in the lounge filled with businessmen and pleasure-seekers, master and slave met:

"Mr. Brennan!"

"Mr. Young!"

"Oh—good evening!"

"Very, sir, very!"

The crisis had passed.

They went to bed early to avoid a second encounter. When morning came, Mr. Brennan left the boat, taking another downriver to Vicksburg.

A day later the boat stopped at Memphis. Feeling very much at ease now, Josh stood beside the gangplank, watching passengers and visitors come aboard. Suddenly one greeted him. It was Pullum, the speculator who had sold William at Little Rock.

"Young Bowen! What brings you to Memphis? Heard you'd gone up North again. Like it better down here, heh?"

"Pleasure to see you again, sir. Just thought I'd look over more of your country."

It was hard to get rid of the man. He'd finished his business and wanted to gossip. The talk got around to Little Rock. Pullum mentioned "a Minnis boy" he had sold there.

"Belonged to old Minnis of Jessamine County. Know the boy?"

"Oh, yes," Josh said. "Works at the Little Rock House, I believe. Good porter, that boy."

"Yes, he's a smart one, all right. I made $300 on him."

Now William came strolling by, swinging his cane in his best imitation of a young Southern devil. Over Pullum's shoulder Josh could see his face. Glancing up, William recognized the slaveholder. Josh saw his eyes widen in fright, his body tense. It's all over, Josh thought. But suddenly William relaxed, smiled at Josh and, to his horror, instead of retreating quietly to some far corner of the boat, walked right across Pullum's path so that he would be sure to be seen.

To and fro he paraded, coming so close at times Josh wondered if he meant to ask him for an introduction to Pullum. To Josh's relief, the bell rang at last as a signal to weigh anchor, and Mr. Pullum, bowing politely all around, bid Josh good-bye and left the boat.

As soon as Pullum was out of sight, Josh grabbed William's arm. "Why did you do that? You must be crazy!"

"Not me," said William. "Pullum. These whites all crazy when it come to niggers. Sure, I was scared sick when I see him. But then I know he never look at me—dressed white the way I am—and see the thing he buy and sell."

He laughed, a dry, rattling, joyless sound. They leaned over the rail together, looking back toward the busy shore where Pullum had vanished.

As the boat neared Cincinnati, Josh gave William his last instructions. He was to get off first, and alone. A man would be waiting for him. It would be Levi Coffin, and Josh described him to William. They would drive off to Levi's place, outside the city.

"What happen then?"

"I don't know exactly," Josh said. "The Coffins will talk it over with you, see what you want to do. You could stay in Cincinnati and look for work, though that's taking a chance. Or you could move on North."

"That what I like! Never be satisfied till I get a good space between me and Kentucky. But how will I go? Where will I go?"

"Don't worry about that, William. The Coffins will help. If you do head North, they'll send you on to another agent up the line."

"Who would that be?"

"I don't know. I never ask, and they wouldn't tell me if I did. The idea is to keep as few people as possible knowing who the agents are. Each man or woman along the way knows perhaps only the next one he has passed people on to. That way if any one of them gets into trouble, he can't be tricked or forced into giving a lot of names he doesn't know."

William nodded. "I'll see you again at the Coffins'?"

"No," said Josh. "I won't be following you there."

"What you be doing then?"

"I'm going back to Kentucky."

"Back!" William shook his head. "That not good," he said. "You forget Pullum see you on this boat? He sure to hear about me getting away. And he'll be mad. Then he think a minute and he say, 'I see that Josh Bowen on the same boat!' He put that all together and he begin to suspicion something wrong. If you go back, somebody be watching you, man. And that not good!"

"It doesn't worry me," Josh said. "Sure, Pullum saw me, but no one knows *you* escaped on the same boat. And besides, if I show up in Kentucky right quick, they'll figure I haven't anything to worry about or I wouldn't be back there."

William looked doubtful. "They not dumb, Josh," he said. "Mean as hell, but not dumb."

The whistle blew, and the boat began poking its way toward the shore.

10

Slave Stealer

The Coffins reached him in Kentucky with a message asking him to help a sixteen-year-old girl held in Covington. Emily Ward had been sold to slave traders, who were keeping her in an attic fronting on the Ohio until they could take her down to New Orleans for delivery to a house of prostitution that catered to whites. It was arranged for Josh to come late at night, when the moon was down. Emily had a rope of blankets ready, and when she lowered it from the window, he sent up boy's clothes. She changed into them quickly and slid down. At the river there was a big log lying halfway in the water, and, getting astride it with two boards, they paddled silently across the Ohio.

A message once traveled up the grapevine from state to state until it reached Boston, then wound back down south along another route, all the way to Josh in Kentucky. And when he decoded it, he found the cry for help had originated only a few miles from where he was—Carter and Vinette Rhoads, with their three boys, were ready to escape from a farm near Lexington. A messenger brought Josh the mother's headkerchief and a spoon bent in a peculiar way—signs of identification which would mean to the Rhoads that whoever came to help could be trusted.

He reached the farm, telling the few people he encountered that he was a miller looking for work. He wandered over to the shed where Rhoads and two of his boys were busy making shoes. Josh immediately took out the headkerchief and wiped his face with it. Rhoads, a short, stocky man with skin almost blue-black, glanced at him, said nothing. Josh got sociable and twenty minutes later pulled the spoon from his pocket and asked for a hammer to straighten it out.

Rhoads appeared unmoved. He sent the two boys out, then instantly told Josh to meet him and his wife in an open field that night. Josh drifted off.

The night was dark and cloudy. At ten o'clock Rhoads appeared alone. He led Josh a few rods off, and suddenly his wife stepped out from behind a tree. They talked for fifteen minutes. While they made their plans, Rhoads watched for trouble, kneeling, face to the ground, arms sprawled, head cocked back—a position that helps a man see better in the dark. His wife did not call Josh "master" nor did she say "sir," by which he knew she had confidence in him. They agreed to meet the next night, two miles from the farm. It was too risky for Josh to be seen again close by.

He spent the next day walking from one grist mill to another, asking for work. At the hour set, all five of the family were there in the woods. They started out, traveling by compass and a bull's-eye lantern at night and hiding in the cedars by day.

For four days and nights they were on the way, raiding cornfields and outdoor ovens, and milking cows. To warm themselves they made small fires by rubbing flint rocks together so the sparks could ignite cornstalks they had gathered.

At last the river. They improvised a raft from the side of an old shed. Before dawn they were safely inside a free home in Ohio, the first stop on the trail of the North Star.

Josh came to know Kentucky better than his own face. He learned what caves and riverbanks to hide in, which woods were the thickest, where abandoned sheds and barns offered shelter. He got to know every trap and every trick to get around it. As he told the

Coffins, the mechanics of escape were simple enough. But day after day he lived with the fear of failure, of discovery. So long as it did not paralyze action, it helped, for his nerves had to be strung tight if his mind and body were to perform with the speed and strength emergencies demanded. One little mistake could be terrible in its consequences for the slaves. The danger for them was more than capture: it was flogging; it was being sold to the South; it was death.

RAN AWAY—MY NEGRO MAN, RICHARD

A REWARD OF TWENTY-FIVE DOLLARS WILL BE PAID FOR HIS APPREHENSION, DEAD OR ALIVE! SATISFACTORY PROOF WILL ONLY BE REQUIRED OF HIS BEING KILLED. HE HAS WITH HIM, IN ALL PROBABILITY, HIS WIFE ELIZA, WHO RAN AWAY FROM COLONEL THOMPSON.

ABNER RAMSAY

TWO HUNDRED DOLLARS REWARD

RAN AWAY FROM THE SUBSCRIBER, A CERTAIN NEGRO NAMED BEN (COMMONLY KNOWN BY THE NAME OF BEN FOX). ALSO, ONE OTHER NEGRO, BY THE NAME OF RIGDON, WHO RAN AWAY ON THE 8th OF THIS MONTH.

> I WILL GIVE THE REWARD OF ONE HUNDRED
> DOLLARS FOR EACH OF THE ABOVE NEGROES, TO
> BE DELIVERED TO ME OR CONFINED IN THE COUNTY
> JAIL, OR FOR THE KILLING OF THEM, SO THAT I
> CAN SEE THEM.
>
> W D COBB

Most of the slaves he helped could not read. But they knew what these posters meant. And still they fled.

Helen Payne was one. She was an old woman he met on a road outside Maysville one day, with carpetbag in her hand. She looked to be over eighty, her face a deep-polished mahogany, her hands curled into claws by rheumatism, but her walk still firm. She moved with deliberation, as though planning where to put each step. She was singing softly to herself. He swung in beside her, slowing his pace, trying to catch the words of her song:

> *Ole Satan is one busy ole man;*
> *He roll dem blocks all in my way;*
> *But Jesus is my bosom friend;*
> *He roll dem blocks away.*

In a while she told him, "I prayed to God for freedom for a long time, but nothing come of it. So then I say, 'Jesus waitin for *you*. Legs! Give me freedom!' And they answer my prayer."

He couldn't understand her complete trust. Why should she tell him, a stranger, and a white man? Then as she talked on, he saw she seemed to do everything out of an inner sense of rightness, an instinctive feeling for the time, the place, the enemy, the ally.

She had two children and nine grandchildren still living on the plantation. She had dreamed of freedom for a long time. But not until now had she been able to make the attempt. She had figured out one plan after another and always discarded them. She knew nothing of the world outside. How could she expect to succeed? Wouldn't her flight cast suspicion on the family she left behind? Suppose they were sold off!

As the years passed she gave up plotting and turned to faith. Something, somebody, would turn up and make her free. It never happened. Then one night, lying in the dark, it suddenly came to her that she had very few years left to live. And she could not bear the thought of dying in slavery. She was filled with grief at the thought of leaving her family. But now her mind was clear, and a deep calm settled over her spirit. Nothing would make her give up the thought of flight. On the next Sunday, the day the slaves were allowed to rest or to visit friends on other plantations, she was ready. She had hidden a little bundle of clothing some distance from the cabin. She put a piece of bread in her pocket, and with a last look at the cabin and the children playing near the door, she walked away. She was so old, she said, she felt no one would bother her if they saw her walking on the road. So she had simply headed north. And two hours later Josh had come up beside her. As they walked on together Josh glanced behind them from time to time. But the way was clear. He was amazed at how serene she was, how confident that now at last was her time to be free and nothing could interfere.

They boarded a steamer, Josh pretending to be her master, and proceeded to Pittsburgh. There an abolitionist editor took over the responsibility of finding her a home and friends.

Slave after slave disappeared across the Ohio. The slaveholders in Mason County along the river's edge were frantic. They formed a society for joint action to protect their property. "Losses by flight are so great," the *Lexington Observer and Reporter* said, "the value of slave property has dropped twenty-five per cent in all the counties bordering on the Ohio River."

Kentucky had to do something. The governor sent two commissioners to the Ohio legislature. Stop your people from interfering with our slave property, they begged. The gentlemen of the legislature were amiable. They wanted nothing to disturb business relations with the friendly state to the south. Nor, for that matter, did they like seeing their neighborhoods becoming places of refuge for runaway blacks.

From now on, said Ohio law, any interference with attempts to arrest a fugitive or to take him back into Kentucky will bring a heavy fine and a prison sentence. To encourage Ohioans to cooperate, Kentucky made it profitable. She offered a handsome reward of $100 to anyone in a free state who caught a fugitive slave and delivered him to his owner in Kentucky, or $75 if the fugitive was brought to a jail anywhere in Kentucky and the owner notified so that he could reclaim his property.

So the risks grew greater. But the flow of fugitives went on. To quiet suspicion, Josh thought he had better shift his work to Montgomery, a county new to him. There, at the foot of the mountains, he came upon an old plantation where cattle and horses were raised. Introducing himself as a circuit preacher, he was welcomed as a guest of the family by Mr. Lockhart, a hearty old man in his seventies, who was lord of the estate.

He soon observed that several of the slaves were so nearly white they could not be distinguished from their master except by dress and short-cut hair. He became interested in Julie, a young slave of about fifteen, who worked in the big house. Gaining her confidence, he learned that she was the fourth in descent from her master. She was the great-great-granddaughter of a slave whom old Lockhart had taken as his mistress when he was sixteen and she fourteen. And now, Julie told him, he had let her know he expected to make her his mistress too.

Josh stayed on for two weeks, long enough to become familiar with the family's habits and to make sure that he could manage an escape for Julie and her mother. They made careful plans to meet one night at the edge of a wood by the road running out of Frenchburg. Both mother and daughter were so fair-skinned it would be easy for the three of them to pose as a family.

He made a quick trip to a distant town to buy good clothing for the two women. At the appointed hour he pulled up in a rented carriage, backed off the road and found them in the trees. But Julie's mother had changed her mind. No argument would

prevail upon her to leave the state. *Her* mother—
and her two other children—were still on the farm,
and she wanted to provide some way for them to
escape. But it was too late for that. Mother and
daughter separated—crying bitterly because they
were likely never to meet again—and, after changing into a stylish dress, Julie took her seat in the
carriage beside Josh and they drove swiftly away.

They reached Lexington the next morning. Pretending to be newlyweds, they took a room in an
outlying inn. Early the next day they caught a train
for Frankfort, where they would board a steamer on
the Kentucky River that would take them to the Ohio
and let them off at Cincinnati. He would bring Julie
to Levi and Kate. They would know what to do next.

It was Julie's first ride on a train. She sat beside
him, staring out the window, her hands rigid in her
lap. Josh had suggested that aboard the train they
act like strangers who had taken seats together by
chance. He could guess what she must be feeling
inside. They still had a way to go before they were
out of this slave state.

He was reading a newspaper when a passenger
coming down the aisle from behind them lurched
against Josh's shoulder as the train went around a
curve. The man murmured an apology. At the sound
of his voice Julie turned her face from the window

and glanced up at the man. Josh could sense the fright that seized her, though she kept her face calm. The man stared hard at her, his forehead wrinkling as though he was trying to place someone he'd once known. He opened his mouth to speak, then shook his head and went on down the swaying aisle. Julie sat there frozen until he had disappeared into the car ahead. Josh opened his paper wide so that it shielded both their faces.

"What is it?" he said in a low voice.

"That man—Lucas Thompson—he manages the place next to ours. Dear God! I thought he'd take me!"

"Don't worry now, Julie. He's gone. Decided he didn't know you after all. When we reach Frankfort we'll get off from the car behind us and avoid seeing him again."

She gave a deep sigh.

"Try to sleep. We've only an hour to go."

She nodded and turned back to the window. Resting her chin on her hand, she closed her eyes. After a while she seemed to be asleep. Josh went back to his paper. He began to feel thirsty. There was no water in their car. He got up to try the car behind. He was taking water from the small tank at the rear when he heard screaming and yelling from the car he had left. Passengers around him shot out of their seats and crowded the aisle, trying to see what was happening up ahead. Josh struggled to get by them. It seemed to take forever before he could make his way into his own car. Just as he entered it the train, which had been slowing down, stopped and began moving backward cautiously. Why? he wondered. His own car was jammed with passengers standing on seats and pushing in the aisle. There was a babble of excited voices. He stood on an empty seat. Where was she? He scanned the car swiftly, looking for her up and down the aisle. No sign of her. Where could she be? What had happened? Sweat broke out on his face, his palms, ran from under his arms down his sides.

Now he could make out what the voices were saying. "Jumped! Right off the train! . . . ran down the aisle when some man came up to her . . . bolted out of her seat . . . they say she just opened the door and leaped right off the train . . . man never even touched her!"

He felt sick in the pit of his stomach. The train was grinding to a stop. Passengers nearest the doors jammed onto the platforms between the cars. As he got to a door he heard groans and cries, a woman's screams, and then the sound of retching. Now he was able to get off and look.

Julie had jumped from the train when it was

passing around the side of a hill. She had leaped on the near side and the steep slope had rolled her back down onto the track and under the moving train. The wheels had sliced over her, killing her at once.

He could figure out what must have happened. Lucas Thompson had gone back to his seat, thought about the face he had seen, and returned either because he knew it was his neighbor's slave running away, or because he wanted another look to make sure it wasn't. Julie had seen him coming toward her and in a panic had fled, jumping off the train in the desperate hope of escaping capture.

The train crew put the mangled body in a bag and stowed it in the freight car. The engine began puffing ahead once more. He sat alone beside the empty seat.

He had failed Julie, and she had died because of it. If he had stayed in his seat, she would not have run, and maybe he could have bluffed their way out of it. Even if Thompson had claimed her as fugitive and she had been taken back into slavery, she would still be alive, and there would be another chance for flight.

It was the only time he had failed, he tried to tell himself. But it gave him no comfort. Having failed once, he knew it could happen again. He turned his face to the window. The deep green woods slowly reeled back, as the train chugged ahead. The canvas bag on the floor of the freight car was all he could see. How could he let her mother know the terrible thing that had happened? Who would bury Julie? He dared not take care of her himself. It would raise too many dangerous questions now. Behind his eyes he felt painful pressure. He closed them, leaning his head back against the seat.

Gradually he sensed someone standing in the aisle, staring down at him. He opened his eyes. It was Lucas Thompson.

"Thought you were asleep," Thompson said.

"Just dozing."

"Mind if I sit here a minute?"

Josh shrugged and moved closer to the window to make room.

Thompson turned to him. "Awful thing that business before."

Josh nodded.

"That poor creature was sitting right here, wasn't she?"

"Yes," said Josh.

"You own her?"

"*Own* her?"

"Yes," said Thompson, "she was a slave, of course. Belonged to a neighbor of mine, old man

Lockhart. I thought I recognized her aboard the train. But I couldn't imagine what she'd be doing riding here. Then I thought maybe the man she was with had just bought her."

"Well, I didn't."

"That beats me! What was she doing on this train then?"

"You can't ask her now," said Josh, struggling to keep his voice matter-of-fact.

"I wonder if she was running away?"

"If she was, she didn't get very far."

"Lockhart's not going to like this piece of news. Had a soft spot for her, he did, one of his favorites. Quite a loss, quite a loss."

"There must be more where she came from."

"Oh, yes," said Thompson. "He's rich. He can afford most any nigger he wants. Got plenty of hens in his barnyard, that old rooster." He chuckled. "Well," he said, getting up, "I'll be going back to my seat. Next stop's mine."

"You'll be letting your friend know about the girl so he can see to her burial?"

"Oh, I'll tell him all right," said Thompson. "But if I know Lockhart, he won't be spending a red cent on her now. 'The railroad killed her,' he'll say. 'Let em bury their dead.' "

He smiled down at Josh, turned and went up the aisle.

At Frankfort, Josh left the train. He found out that if he waited a few hours, he could catch another going back to Lexington.

"Step up, gentlemen! What'll you offer for this lively wench! Warranted sound in mind and body! She'll make you a good cook, washer or ironer. Come gentlemen, bid up on this likely nigger! What do I hear now, what do I hear?"

Josh stood near the rickety auction block. Across the square, the white building faced with pillars was full of droning lawyers and dozing justices. On his return to Lexington the day before, he had seen little knots of people from the countryside standing everywhere, swapping gossip, talking politics and weather and crops and horses. Tomorrow's court day, he realized then. It was a set Monday each month when the justices of the peace sat and folks the country round took the day off.

He had worked his way through streets crowded with farmers' rigs, buggies and surreys, to reach the public square. It was full of bargains—bargains in livestock and clothing, stoves and beds, boxes and plows, harnesses and molasses. Peddlers, junk dealers, medicine men and tooth extractors stood on the fringes, crying their wares and services.

Sooner or later you were bound to meet everyone you knew, watching the bidding at the public auctions on court square, where slaves were sold. Not all the biddable property was put up there. Some planters were squeamish about buying and selling in public. It was better taste to deal in Negroes privately. Still, there was no lack of human bargains to be haggled over, estates to be settled, unclaimed runaways to be disposed of, demands of creditors to be met.

The practiced eye knew what a slave was worth on the market. Buyers judged by physical condition, skill, age, color. A male field hand who was young and strong rated a good bid. Reliability and skill were wanted in a mechanic or servant, in a young woman, health and the ability to bear plenty of children. Looks counted a lot. The lighter her skin, the more attractive she was to the bidders, and slaveholders disposed of such choice stock for a thousand dollars or even twice that. Not when it was a boy or man, however. There a light skin caused the price to drop. Too much of a risk: he could pass as a white and flee more easily.

On this court day, Lexington was buzzing with talk about Talitha.

"Beautiful," a man told Josh. "She is just the most beautiful sixteen-year-old you ever laid eyes on. Only one sixty-fourth African!"

"How come?" Josh asked.

The man leaned closer. "Daughter of her master, that's who. Breckinridge's—one of the best families."

"Why's he want to sell her?"

"He don't!"

"Well, then, who does?"

The man looked at him scornfully. "His wife," he said.

Then, taking pity on so ignorant a young fellow, he told Josh the story. Talitha had been raised in the family as a servant. So fond of her, the master was, he had given her the luxury of an education. She acquired all the grace and manners of her mistress who, hating Talitha almost from birth, now had come to envy her as well.

Jed Breckinridge had fallen deeply into debt, gambling, mostly. He was obliged to sell many of his slaves to satisfy his creditors. A family quarrel broke out, so furious the whole town soon knew about it. The master was refusing to sell Talitha, with the mistress insisting she too must go on the auction block. Who had won became public that very morning when the list of slaves to be sold on the following court day, a month hence, was slapped up on walls everywhere. There, in the middle, was Talitha's name.

A tremendous idea lodged in Josh's mind almost before the man had finished his story. He pushed his way down to Short Street, where slaves to be sold were kept in a trader's jail. Looking like any other buyer come to inspect, he was let in. There was no bench or table in the large room. Some of the slaves sat on the floor with chin resting on hand, eyes staring vacantly, bodies rocking back and forth in motion that never stopped. Others moved restlessly about, stopped, leaned against the wall, walked up and down again. Only a few wept. He wondered if it was because the place was too public and the dealers too near. He saw children huddled in a corner, the youngest scarcely fifteen days old cradled in a little girl's arms.

A speculator came in. He asked for slaves named on a list in his hand. When they were lined up for him, he examined them carefully. He pulled open each mouth so that the teeth could be seen. He pinched legs and arms to test the muscles. He walked them up and down to detect signs of lameness, then made them stoop and bend various ways to see if there were concealed wounds or ruptures. He inspected backs and buttocks for signs of whippings. Men, women, boys, girls—it made no difference.

Josh looked for Talitha, but no one of her description was to be seen. By discreet questioning he learned she was kept in a private room above. Now he knew what she was intended for. This was the room for "fancy girls." They were held apart for discriminating buyers to examine as prospective mistresses. Everyone in the South knew Lexington specialized in this "choice stock." It was a favorite resort for horse-breeders, turfmen, planters and gamblers. And color was no barrier when it came to their personal pleasure.

Better not ask to be shown the choice stock. It would call too much attention to himself. Casually he strolled off, checked out of his boardinghouse, and hurried away to Levi Coffin's.

11

The Auction Block

"But there's little risk, Levi!" And Josh went over it once more, slowly, patiently, ramming home his point. "First, we raise a large enough sum, so we're sure we can make the try. Meanwhile, time's working for us. The excitement will be building up all by itself. If you'd only been with me on court day! The crowds, they were enormous. Slave sales go on all the time, but court day's something special. The choice stock—the slaves that promise to get the highest prices—are held in reserve for court day, because that's when speculators show up from all over the South. That story I heard about Talitha spread through the town like wildfire. What was going on in the Breckinridge family was once only quiet gossip. Now it's right out in the open, a public scandal about one of the best bluegrass families. By next court day there won't be a dealer in the South who won't know all about Talitha. You can be sure they'll be in Lexington to put in their bids.

"Now, here's what we should do. We find a way to tip off Northern editors that something sensational will happen at Lexington that day. They'll be sure to have correspondents there. The bidding on Talitha starts. We wait till it gets hot and high. Then we go in! Just think! When people all over the country pick up their papers and read about what's happening—a white man, a man in high society, a father selling his own daughter at public auction!—how many people will be won over to our side!"

Out of breath, Josh subsided. He had gone over the plan three times now, and each time Levi Coffin saw another reason why it wouldn't work.

"Josh," Levi said now, "a minute ago there, you said that after the bidding on Talitha starts, *we* go in. Who's that 'we'? Who'd be doing the bidding in your scheme?"

"I wish it could be me, Levi. Lord, think of it!" Josh paused. "But that would be lunatic."

Kate let out a long sigh of relief. "You could do it all right, Josh, but your face has been seen so often in Kentucky. Someone would recognize you and spoil everything."

"Even if they didn't," said Josh, "and I succeeded, it would still be bad. So much attention would be fixed on me it'd hurt my usefulness in the future."

Levi wasn't satisfied. "You or somebody else, Josh, it'd still be a huge risk and reason enough to say no. But there's the matter of the money, too."

"But we only have to go out and raise it!"

"Only!" Levi was indignant. "Do you have any idea what it will cost? More cash than a farmer around here makes in years! Who's got money like that? And if anyone has it, who'd give it up for a half-baked scheme like yours?"

"Oh come, Levi!" It was Kate. "You *do* know men with pockets ample enough for this. Lawyer Chase, for one. And what about Nicholas Longworth? Both of them right here in Cincinnati! They've given money many a time for good reason. And what better reason than this?"

"Kate," said Levi, "don't you start talking as though I'm against Talitha. I want to see that girl saved as much as any other slave. But it has to be a practical idea, an idea that has a large chance of success. Otherwise, it's wrong to risk someone else's money—and maybe someone else's life—on it."

Nobody said a word for a long time.

Then Levi pushed away from the table. "Got to see to the animals," he said. He went out the door.

I've lost, Josh thought. His eyes closed, and he slumped in his chair, fighting an overwhelming desire to sleep.

"Wait, Josh," said Kate. "He needs time to think. Does it best when he's milking."

Half an hour later, the door opened.

"Kate," said Levi, "pack the carpetbag. For two. That Nick Longworth has never been able to say no to you."

Before they could get down from the rig, Josh was at them.

"We got it, Josh! All it should take!" Now Levi was as excited as Josh had been.

"Was it hard? You've been gone three days—I haven't been able to eat!"

"No," said Levi. "It was a lot easier than I expected. I got to Salmon Chase first. Figured if he'd go along, a solid lawyer like that, then Longworth might come in too. Chase saw right away"— "Quicker than you did, Levi," Kate put in—"what an effect on public opinion this might have. Reporters describing a slave auction, then the climax—the sale of a young woman, put on the block by her white father. 'I'll put up half the money myself,' Chase said. But we had to wait another day for Longworth to get back from a business trip."

"We went to see him in that beautiful house," said Kate. She sighed. "What money that man puts into furniture and paintings! He's a strange one. Now Salmon Chase is a man you can predict. He gives so much of his time to defending fugitive slaves. But that Nick Longworth—one day he's promoting laws to drive blacks out of town, and the next he's handing over money to save their lives."

"Lucky thing this was one of his good days," said Levi. "It usually is, when Kate sets to work on him. He promised us not only the rest of the money but insisted on taking care of the newspapers, too. Let a man like Longworth snap his fingers, and they jump, all right."

"Well now," said Josh, his mind running ahead, "who'll we find to do the bidding?"

"We have the man," said Levi. "Noah Tyler, one of Longworth's clerks. Very responsible fellow, they tell me. Longworth asked him then and there, and he said yes."

"You don't look quite so pleased now," said Kate.

"Oh, I am," said Josh. "Just gave me a start, to think of a clerk carrying out this job."

"But you'll be there, too," Levi said. "If anything goes wrong, you are to rush word to Longworth."

On the Sunday before court day, Josh traveled to Lexington. He took a room at the small tavern agreed upon, then walked about the town. The day was warm and clear, the streets crowded with visitors, some from as far away as Boston and New Orleans. The afternoon dragged by. A little before six, he was back at the tavern. He went into the bar. Some men were standing at the rail drinking, and a few others sat at tables, reading the newspapers. Promptly as the clock on the wall struck the hour, Josh took a red handkerchief out of his pocket and blew his nose. A tall man of about forty got up from a table and walked toward Josh, bearing a dignified paunch before him. Coming close, he let his newspaper slip from under his arm. As the man bent to pick it up, he glanced into Josh's face, then straightened up, walked out past the desk and up the stairs. Noah Tyler, of course. They were not to speak to each other. Josh followed Tyler up the stairs. Just as he reached the top, he saw Tyler's boot kicking the door to room 4 closed.

His own room, 7, was down the hall. He went in, took off his shoes and flopped on the bed. The stale sheets gave off a sour smell. His eyes wandered over the ceiling and rested on a spider dangling from the beam. He moved a bit to the right just in case the thread should snap. What was Tyler doing now? Was he nervous? Must be, with so much money on him. He wondered if the man was an abolitionist. Unlikely—Longworth didn't pick his clerks for that reason. Or his friends. But Tyler must be reliable. . . .

Josh turned his thoughts to Talitha. Today again he'd heard men talking about Breckinridge's girl— her astonishingly light eyes, her rich olive skin, her long black hair, how much she looked like her master. . . .

After a while he dozed off. About an hour later he jerked awake, unable to realize for a moment where he was. His belly rumbled with hunger. He pulled on his shoes and went downstairs to have supper. Only two men at the tables, and no sign of Tyler. Must have eaten already, he thought. He finished his meal and went out to sit on the porch. Two horsemen trotted by in elegant riding clothes, and then a wagon rumbled down the street. He could hear the sounds of the busy town carried on the spring wind. If only *he* were going about this business tomorrow, not some clerk who'd never lifted his eyes from those columns of figures. This was work for an experienced man! How could they trust it to a fellow who'd spent his whole life hiding behind a wicket?

He kept an eye out for Tyler, but the man never appeared. Sticking to his room? About eleven o'clock Josh went up to bed. He must have been asleep for hours when he heard a racket in the hall. He held his watch to the window, squinting at the hands. Three-thirty. Then the wall of his room shook as a heavy body caromed off it. He heard a voice cursing incoherently. He jumped out of bed and, opening his door a crack, peered out. His nose wrinkled, taking in the strong smell of sour mash. Down the hall Noah Tyler was fumbling with his key at the lock of his door. As Josh watched, Tyler dropped the key, kneeled ponderously to find it and fell over on his face, too drunk to keep his balance. He lay sprawled there as though he were falling asleep. Then he began groping for the key, found it and, pulling himself up by holding onto the knob, managed to get the door unlocked. He staggered into his room. A long minute later the lock clicked shut.

Josh closed his own door quietly and got back into bed. He lay there in the dark, thinking about Tyler and tomorrow.

Suddenly he knew what he had to do. When he fell asleep an hour later, the way to do it was clear in his mind. Before dawn he rose, dressed hastily, pulled up his window and stepped out onto the roof of the porch that ran the length of the tavern. He tiptoed to the third window down, found it open as he'd expected and peered in. Noah Tyler was lying belly down on the bed, face toward the opposite wall. He was snoring softly into his pillow. Josh examined the room. Tyler's clothes were heaped on the one chair, standing close by the bed. And then he saw it—a small bag, half-hidden beneath the clothes. He raised the window slowly, wincing at the squeaks. Tyler did not stir. He stepped through, moved to the chair and eased the bag out from under the clothes. Just as he tucked it under his arm there was a loud groan from the bed. Josh stiffened; his arms and legs suddenly turned to lead. Tyler, his back still to Josh, reached down with one hairy arm and yanked the top sheet over his head. A second later the rhythmic snoring resumed.

Josh inched toward the window, put the bag gently down on the porch roof, then climbed out, picked up the bag and began to move back toward the window of his room. He was putting his hand on the sill when he heard the front door below him bang open against the wall and saw a man come down the porch steps. What if he looks up and sees me! Josh sank silently to his knees, making himself as small as possible, stuffing the bag behind him. He felt the sweat pouring from his armpits. The man reached the street, looked one way and then the other, as though uncertain which direction to turn. Standing still, the man pulled out a pipe with one hand, then a tobacco pouch with the other. He filled the pipe carefully, tamping it down till it was just right, then felt for a match. Nothing in this pocket. Or that. He'll turn and go back for a match and see me squatting up here! Josh thought. The man hesitated, shook his head reproachfully, stuck the unlit pipe between his teeth and walked up the street.

Josh stayed kneeling a few seconds more, then, trying to rise to climb through his window, felt as stiff and creaky as if he'd been locked in that position for an hour. He managed to get inside and sank onto his bed. He did not move until his drumming heart had slowed. Then he reached down and opened the bag. Clothes—two shirts, socks, handkerchiefs, razor, comb, tiny mirror, soap, Bible— where was it! Under Tyler's pillow? In his mattress? Why hadn't he thought of that? His throat went dry, his heart hammered again. He threw everything in the bag on the floor, held it upside down, shook it. Nothing more fell out. He dropped the bag on the floor beside him and let his head hang over the edge of the bed, eyes closed, hating himself for being such a fool. How would he ever explain this? One eye opened, looked idly down into the mouth of the bag. He grabbed at it suddenly. There was new stitching along one side. He yanked out his pocketknife, ripped the thread open and thrust his hand into the newly made pocket. His fingers touched crackly paper. Out came a thin wad of bills. He turned his back to the window and counted: twenty hundreds and several tens. Tears of relief came to his eyes. Then he thought of Noah Tyler waking up in a hour or two, finding his bag gone. Good God, the drunken fool will likely want to kill himself.

He allowed himself to feel bad only for a minute. Then he transferred the contents of Tyler's bag to his own, stuffing the bag itself in, too. He went downstairs, paid his bill and began walking toward Court Square. On the way, he got rid of Tyler's clothes and bag. The sun was up now and the day warm and clear. He took breakfast and reached Cheapside as the auction was about to start.

The square was packed with at least two thousand people. He pushed his way to the front as far as he could, so his bids would not be overlooked. Chatting with the entry clerks, whose desks were next to the block, was the auctioneer. He was a skinny old man in a fork-tailed coat, plaid vest and calfskin boots, with a broad-brimmed white beaver hat pushed far back on his head. Now he stepped up on the auction block.

"Gentlemen," he began, "I'm going to sell you this morning some of the likeliest niggers as ever you've seen put up. They are sold for no fault, and every one of em is warranted. But look at em for yourself. *You*-all know good niggers. You'll see there ain't a single lot you won't want to own."

A "lot" proved to be any number from one slave to a full family. The auctioneer had a slave to assist him, who brought the blacks to the stand and exercised them to display their points to the bidders. As soon as one lot was sold, the assistant went off to bring up another. At last it was Talitha. Trembling before the staring crowd, she looked hopelessly down at her feet.

"Look up, girl, look up!" the auctioneer commanded. Then he turned to the crowd:

"Gentlemen, this is a very choice specimen— a very likely girl, warranted sound in every respect, and the title is perfect! She's tiptop, she is, and threatens to become magnificently prolific! What will you give for her, how much? Do I hear $250? Only $250 for this superb piece of property?"

The bids went up fast by twenty-fives and fifties to $500, $600, $700. Josh glanced away from Talitha and saw a hand waving from the front ranks of the crowd around the auction block. He squinted into the sun. It was Noah Tyler, trying to catch his eye. Josh waved back. Tyler took out his wallet, held it above his head and opened it out to show it was empty, shaking his head all the while. Josh nodded and put on a mournful expression, to show he understood. He'll soon know what happened, he thought.

"$700!" the auctioneer was chanting, "$700 for this magnificent article—something that no respectable man can do without. A superb piece of property going off at a sacrifice! Going at a dead loss! How much am I bid? That's it, I see you sir, $750 is bid, $800, $800, couldn't think of selling such a beautiful nigger at such a rate! Did you say $850? $900 it is! $900—that looks something like business, go it, gentlemen! And see who'll get tired first, you or me. Keep at her! Nothing like progress—this is an age of progress—what have you got up over there? $1000? $1000 did I hear? $1000 it is! Go on, go on, gentlemen, now you're doing it!"

Rattling off figures and sputtering his short phrases the auctioneer swept the crowd with his glance, watching for the smallest nod or look of assent, all the while talking, gesturing, moving, clapping his hands.

At $1000 Josh was about to go in, when an elegant middle-aged man standing in the front row cut in and cried, "Send her this way!"

The auctioneer paused, evidently recognizing the new bidder. "Walk out there, now," he said to Talitha, "step lively for the man from New Orleans!" The bidder turned the girl round and round, told her to grin and show her teeth, pushing her lips aside with his fingers, and then examined her closely from head to foot, seeming to enjoy the crowd's attention upon himself as much as the inspection of Talitha. Josh saw that some in the crowd were angry at this, but others openly relished the display. Before the man could wave the girl back to the auctioneer, Josh yelled out, "$1050!"

The auctioneer pulled Talitha away from the man from New Orleans and faced her toward Josh. New Orleans was angry. "$1100!" he called.

"$1150," came a voice from the rear of the crowd.

"$1200!" Josh said.

"$1200 it is!" said the auctioneer. "That's it—encourage true merit—don't be looking over there, sir—if you don't mind what you're about, you'll lose your chance! You'll let her slip through your fingers! Do I hear $1250?"

The bids raced up to $1300, $1350, $1400. The crowd's attention was switching from Talitha to Josh. It was astonishing to find so young a bidder, and in these special circumstances of Talitha's sale. Besides, he neither acted nor spoke like a Southerner.

By now everyone was dropping out but the man from New Orleans and Josh. When the bidding reached $1400, New Orleans called out arrogantly, "How high you plan to bid, boy?"

"Higher than you, sir," he replied. Cheers from the crowd. They liked a race, any kind of race.

The bids rose by smaller steps now. Josh was remembering that the crisp new bills in his breast pocket were not his own. The auctioneer grew impatient, tried to push them. "Why, gentlemen, I'm really astonished at your backwardness! This girl is none of your everyday niggers! She's a specimen that some of your abolitionists would give almost any price for. But they shan't have her!"

And the bids rose to $1500. Again Josh's enemy, shrugging his shoulders nervously asked, "How high are you going?"

And again he said, "Higher than you do, sir."

They continued to bid, slowly, carefully—$1520, $1530, $1540—inching up the price. Talitha was almost forgotten by the crowd, fixed on the duel between the man from New Orleans and this young outlander. The older man—gambler? turfman? certainly no nigger-trader—was a type they knew well, always ready to spend high for Lexington's "choice stock." But this young man, this ill-dressed stranger, who was he? Yankee? Where did he get this kind of money? And what did he want with Talitha?

The auctioneer was angry now. Josh leaped to $1575 and the man from New Orleans was silent. The hammer rose, paused, lowered, rose, fell, and then the exasperated auctioneer, dropping his hammer, suddenly seized Talitha, unbuttoned her dress, threw it back from her shoulders and exposed her breasts to the crowd, crying, "Look here, gentlemen! Who is going to lose such a chance as this! Here is a girl fit to be the mistress of a king!"

Cries of anger and disgust rose from some among the crowd. "Shame! Shame!" But the old auctioneer knew his rights and was not to be stopped. Again he called out for bids.

"$1600," said New Orleans.

"$1625," Josh called.

There was another pause, and the auctioneer, eager to pump up the bidding, suddenly turned the girl's back to the crowd and, lifting up her skirt, bared her body from her feet to her waist.

"Ah, gentlemen," he cried out, slapping her flesh, "who is going to be the winner of this prize? What is the next bid?"

The crowd was in an uproar now.

"$1650!" New Orleans cried out.

The hammer rose high, quivered, lowered. "Are you all done?" said the auctioneer, waving his hammer in the air. "Once—twice—do I hear more? Three—" and his hammer trembled, as the man from New Orleans flushed with triumph. Talitha looked appealingly to Josh. "Three—" and the hammer fell slowly.

"$1700!" Josh yelled.

"17–17–17—the girl is going—going—" and to New Orleans, "Are you going to bid again, sir?" New Orleans shook his head slowly.

"Going at $1700 once, $1700 twice, $1700 going, going, gone to cash for $1700!" cried the auctioneer, crashing his hammer down as Talitha crumpled in a faint.

"You've got her damned cheap, sir!" the auctioneer called to Josh over the heads of the crowd.

"And what's the boy going to do with her?" It was the man from New Orleans, furious and sneering, addressing himself to the crowd.

"Free her!" Josh cried out. Groans mixed with cheers.

He leaped to the platform, helped Talitha to her feet and led her down. At the bottom they stopped by one of the entry clerks. People pressed close to see if the young stranger really had that much money. Josh reached into his pocket and took out the roll of crisp bills. As he began to peel off the hundreds, Noah Tyler pushed in.

"By God, boy!" he said, eyes blazing. He grabbed Josh's arm as though he meant to wrench the money away.

"Mr. Tyler," Josh said coolly, "will you kindly see to the lady here? While I pay my obligation?"

Tyler closed his mouth and gave his arm to Talitha, who looked wonderingly from one man to the other. Josh finished counting out the money, handed it to the clerk, and received Talitha's bill of sale in return. Then the three of them moved off through the crowd.

"By God, boy!" said Tyler angrily, starting in again, talking over the bewildered Talitha, who walked in trembling fear between them. "You're a wild man! Orders mean nothing to you? Do as you like, eh? Even to thieving!"

"I'm sorry to have scared you," Josh said. "But the money was for the girl, not you and not me. I saw you come in last night. I had to take the chance. I couldn't trust you'd be able to show up here today and carry out your part."

Tyler flushed. "I meant to have only a shot or two. But everyone was standing rounds, and before I knew it . . ."

"Let's forget it," said Josh. "Now we have to get

away from here." They reached the far side of the square and took a carriage to the railroad station. Josh had estimated how long the auction might take and knew they could catch the train for Frankfort with a little wait. It was the same train Josh had taken with Julie scarcely a month ago. He fell silent as they boarded it and was glad Talitha understood they could not talk freely in such close quarters. Once safely on the boat, he found a quiet corner and explained to Talitha who they were, and why Josh had bought her. She moved from tears to hysterical laughter, unable for a long time to believe she was not in a dream.

In a few days, with the help of Chase and Longworth, Talitha was sent to a New England school to finish her education.

News accounts of the auction—a father selling off his own daughter—caused a sensation. Many Northern papers used it as an example of how the slave system brutalized both master and slave. Some defensive Southern editors said it was an extraordinary affair and not likely to happen again. Others denied any such thing ever happened and accused abolitionists of staging it to make propaganda.

Josh's guess proved correct. Talitha's auction

shocked the sleeping conscience of Northerners and made new converts to abolition.

"But," said Levi Coffin, "so will my guess prove correct. Show your face again in Kentucky, Josh, and they'll have a new convert to prison."

12

Escape and Capture

He stood before Kate's mirror, trimming his beard. It had come in thick and curly, as black as the hair on top of his head. "Let it grow any longer," Kate had said, "and you'll look like one of the prophets." It was at the Coffins' insistence that Josh had grown it in the first place. He needed a disguise. A beard was the easiest way to do it. It had seemed to take forever for that first stubble to get anywhere, and now it was so long and luxuriant he had to cut it or people would be casting second glances at a man his age sporting an old-timer's beard. "Besides," Kate had said, "there'll be company tonight, and I wish you'd try to look a bit more human."

When he came downstairs, there she was, the company. Sitting like a queen in Levi's big armchair. Before he could cross the room she rose, hand out, introducing herself.

"Joshua Bowen," she said, smiling, "I'm Deborah Walker. You don't know me, but we've already met."

We couldn't have, he thought. How would any man forget so handsome a woman? Enormous green eyes, full mouth, a mass of copper hair, and a warm, firm handshake.

She saw he was puzzled, and laughed. "It was in Lexington," she said, "scarcely two months ago. I think you were too occupied with Talitha to notice me. I was standing in the crowd."

He was glad he hadn't, or he wouldn't have been able to keep his mind on business.

"I know you live in Lexington," he said. "Levi and Kate told me. But I was under strict instructions not to look you up."

Deborah was as lovely as Kate had said. It was hard to think of her as running any risks. Elegant dress, charming manners, only a trace of her Vermont upbringing in her cultivated voice. She looked and acted just like the daughters of Kentucky's prosperous planters. She had to, he knew, for as the head of the Lexington Female Academy, she enjoyed the favor of the wealthiest people, whose children she taught. She had studied at Oberlin, the Ohio college which had pioneered in taking in women, and in accepting black students on the same basis with whites. By the time she'd graduated, the Coffins had said, she was an ardent abolitionist. Concealing her convictions, she had found a job teaching in Lexington and because of her superior intelligence had rapidly risen to be headmistress of the school.

But all of it was an elaborate cover for her real purpose in going to Kentucky—to help free slaves. The Coffins had come to know her when she was at Oberlin. Once she left for Kentucky, however, they never allowed themselves to be seen in public with Deborah on her rare visits to Ohio. When she needed to communicate with them, she sent letters under an assumed name.

Supper that evening was a rare delight for Josh. He said little, listening to Deborah's revelations of a side of Kentucky life he had never been part of— the world of fashion, of racing, of politics. She had fitted herself perfectly into that world. It was natural that the slaveholders should like and trust her.

The meal over, the talk turned to what had led Deborah to pay this visit. There was a black family in Lexington named Hawkins. The wife, Harriet, and their ten-year-old son, Joe, belonged to a man who had hired out Mrs. Hawkins to do the cleaning in Deborah's school. Lloyd, her husband, was owned by another man, who hired him out as a waiter in the fashionable Phoenix Hotel.

"Harriet's been at the school since before me,"

said Deborah. "She did her work very well but we never talked much. In fact, I avoid any familiarity with slaves nearby so as not to draw suspicion upon me. But a few months ago I noticed Harriet was growing absent-minded, making mistakes, falling into fits of melancholy. Finally I asked her if something was wrong. At first she put me off. But the way she acted became more erratic almost day by day. Everyone was noticing it. So I took her aside again and tried once more to gain her confidence. This time she burst into tears, and the story came out. Her master had died recently, and his heirs were talking about selling off his slaves. That meant she and Joe would almost certainly be separated from her husband. To make things worse, Lloyd's hiring-out time was almost up, and a hotel in Louisville was offering his master a better price for his services. So either way, they faced separation. She cried desperately. But she didn't ask me to do anything. Simply unburdened herself because I was sympathetic."

"What did you tell her?" asked Kate.

"Nothing, at first. I don't have the money to buy their freedom. Nor did I want to ask one of my rich friends to buy them so they could stay together. Maybe someone would have, because both Lloyd and Harriet are young—not quite thirty yet—and excellent workers. But I don't want my patrons to think I have any special interest in slaves.

"The only solution was for them to run away. But how? What chance would three of them have? And should I risk exposing myself by helping someone who worked at the school?

"Then one day, right in the middle of a class, the answer popped into my mind. It was as though someone else had been working hard on it and slipped the solution to me when I wasn't looking. I was so excited I could barely finish the class."

"I know what you mean," said Josh. "That's happened to me, too. You've about given up on finding your way to someplace, and then bang! the map with all the routes posted is right there in your head."

"So you've got the answer," said Levi. "And I suppose we're part of it?"

Deborah smiled. "Maybe," she said. "It depends."

"If it depends on *me*," Josh said, "it's done!"

"Wait a minute, there," said Kate. "Let's find out what *is* to be done."

Two weeks later a bearded young gentleman appeared at David Glass's highly respectable boardinghouse on Second Street in Lexington and took a room. He registered as Calvin Fairfield of Rochester, New York. He mentioned that he would be in town representing his father's farm tool company. At supper that night he sat next to Miss Deborah Walker. The other boarders noticed how charmed by each other these young people were. Within a few days they were lingering in the parlor evenings, chatting amiably, and by the weekend they were out riding together. Ten days after Mr. Fairfield's arrival, it was plain a whirlwind courtship was going on. Miss Walker hardly had time to prepare for her classes, and Mr. Fairfield was obviously neglecting his business. Their display of affection became so open one boarder offered to take bets they would be married before the racing season was over.

Late on the fourth Saturday after Mr. Fairfield's arrival—it was the last day of the races—the young man rented a two-horse hack from Parker Craig's livery stable. At seven in the evening he stopped at Glass's place. Miss Walker had been busy packing a bag. When Mr. Glass teasingly asked if she were going to elope, she blushed but wouldn't say yes or no. As soon as the hack drove up, she dashed out of the house and climbed in.

"Anybody say anything?" asked Josh.

"Just what we expected. They think we're running off to get married."

"Maybe we should!"

"Some other time," said Deborah. "We have other things to do right now."

The horses took the road for Paris. But as the hack came to the edge of Lexington, it veered off in the dark, down a country lane. Half a mile down the road, Josh pulled up under a thick clump of trees. Deborah jumped down, Josh handing her the bag she had packed. She disappeared among the trees. A few minutes later, she came out with three people. They were the Hawkins family, dressed now in the new clothing Deborah had brought. Harriet was heavily veiled and Lloyd wore a cloak with a hood he could draw up to cover his face. If stopped, they were to pass as a white gentleman and lady, and their little servant.

They drove all night, reaching the village of Washington about four in the morning. They were only a few miles from the Ohio, but it was wiser to stop now and hide for the day. When night came they drove on to Maysville and without any difficulty boarded the night ferry and crossed the river to the Ohio side. They galloped to Ripley, where they delivered the three slaves to the Reverend John Rankin, an abolitionist who would speed them on to Canada. Several whites had seen them along the way, but none gave any sign of noticing anything peculiar.

Now Deborah and Josh started back for Lexington, moving fast, hoping to reach town before they were missed. If asked about an elopement, they would laugh it off; they had only gone to visit friends.

They were passing through Paris on Monday night—having covered 156 miles in forty-eight hours—when four horsemen darted out from the trees ahead of them and blocked the road. Josh pulled hard on the reins and brought the hack to a stop. He glanced at Deborah. She was staring straight ahead at the men, her face a deadly white, but she put one steady hand on his arm, as though to reassure him. One of the men had pistols out, pointing at them, while the others dismounted and ran up to the hack. Ordering Josh and Deborah out, they looked in, then tore up the front and back seats.

"Hell!" said one of them. "Ain't no niggers here. Got rid of them, they have."

"What are you talking about?" said Josh. "What niggers?"

"Don't mess with us!" said the man with the pistols. "I'd just as soon kill a nigger-stealer here and now, as see you hung later."

"Who are you?" asked Deborah.

"Deputies," said the leader. "Been on your track since Sunday morning. Posses out everywhere soon as that nigger Lloyd disappeared at the Phoenix House. Sheriff went right to his place and found his woman and his boy gone. Too damn many niggers been run off in these parts. We don't aim to lose any more. Didn't take long to figger out who done it!"

He reached over and yanked fiercely at Josh's beard. The pain was maddening. Tears came to Josh's eyes. He struck at the man's hand. The deputy whipped his pistol across the side of Josh's head, drawing blood and almost cracking his jawbone. Josh groaned and fell back against the hack, nearly fainting.

"Stop it! Stop it!" Deborah cried. She struggled to push the deputy off. "You have no right to hit Mr. Fairfield!"

"Fairfield, is it? That nigger-lover's no more Fairfield than me. Joshua Bowen—that's who he is. And before we're finished with him he'll wish he *was* somebody else!"

Josh was manacled and shoved into the back seat with Deborah. Two deputies tied their horses behind the hack and got up front to drive it into Lexington. At Megowan's jail they were yanked out, Deborah locked in the debtor's cell, and Josh dumped into a slavepen. It was the same jail he had visited the day he came to look for Talitha.

13

I Have Not Broken the Law of Humanity

The heavy door slammed shut, the big key turned in the lock, the footsteps died away.

He was alone.

They had stripped and searched him first. Found nothing incriminating. Then the sheriff had come, asking him to tell how he and Deborah had induced Lloyd and Harriet to run away.

"I have nothing to say," he kept repeating.

"Then don't," said the sheriff. "We've got you without that."

But you haven't, Josh thought. There's no proof we've broken any law. We hadn't been found with slaves. Where's the evidence to indict and convict us? If he kept silent, and Deborah too, nothing might happen to them. He wished he could see her.

His cell was small and dark, but he did not feel isolated. The jail was constantly filling with slaves held for sale. They were kept in two cramped pens nearby. Through the walls he could hear the coming and going.

The next afternoon the sheriff came again.

"Talk now?"

No, he wouldn't.

"All right. What do you think of this?"

He took out a piece of paper and waved it in front of Josh. "This is a copy of a letter we found in your trunk at Glass's. It's in your handwriting. No mistake. It's signed 'Brother' and addressed to 'Dear Sir.' "

Then he read it to Josh. It spoke of plans to fetch Lloyd and his family, and of a "Miss W" who would "cross the river with us."

Could anyone believe he would write such a revealing letter? And if he was stupid enough to do it, why was it sitting in his trunk all the time, and not mailed out?

"What about it?" asked the sheriff. "May as well talk now. We don't need any more 'n this to convict you."

Josh shook his head. And said nothing.

When he was alone again, he thought about this "damning document," as the sheriff called it. It troubled him now. The sheriff had also shown him a newspaper. The editor was advising the jailers to put extra guards on because public opinion was raging so high against the "nigger-stealers" that if the mob could get at them, they would be lynched in the streets.

At such a time, a local jury would be happy to accept any evidence. He knew from the jailer that boarders at Glass's had already told how he and Deborah had often been seen "plotting." And a teacher at the Lexington Female Academy had said she had come into Deborah's office and found her in an "intimate" conversation with Harriet Hawkins.

The letter and such reports were enough. They were speedily indicted for slave-stealing. And on three counts, one for Lloyd, one for Harriet, one for Joe. The maximum punishment on each count was twenty years.

One day a stranger was let into Josh's cell.

"Mr. Bowen?" the man said.

"Who are you?"

"I'm Edmund Nicholas. Our daughter is one of Miss Walker's pupils. A superb teacher, that young lady! I'm sorry to confess we haven't produced any local talent to match her."

"What do you want with me?"

"May I sit down, sir?" And he took a place at one end of the oak bench that was both seat and bed for Josh.

"It's simply this," he went on. "I've been to see Miss Walker, more than once, at her request. She says she is innocent of this charge of slave-stealing. Had nothing whatever to do with it. And I believe her."

Josh was stunned.

He hadn't thought she would talk, what's more lie about what she had done. . . . But how did he know she had? This might be a bluff to draw him out.

As if anticipating what he was thinking, Mr. Nicholas handed him a note. "She said to give you this."

Josh took it. It was in her hand, unmistakably:

Josh—I am innocent, as you know, and I have told everybody of that fact. If you want to help me, you will do as Mr. Nicholas asks.

Deborah

What could she mean? She had shared in the rescue with him; more, it was her own idea. Why was she claiming she was innocent? Silence he would understand. Let the state try to prove her guilt. The burden was on Kentucky. But to *deny* her part?

He handed the note back to Nicholas, trying to keep his hand from trembling.

"This is in Miss Walker's own hand," the man said. "I'm sure you know it. You have my word of honor."

"What of it?" he said.

"Only this. She asks you to confirm her innocence."

"How?"

Mr. Nicholas took out another paper, smoothing it on the bench. "She wants you to sign this. If you do, Miss Walker and her friends are convinced the jury will acquit her."

Josh picked up the paper. He held it in the faint light falling from the window high up in the wall. It bore only one sentence:

> *I do know to a positive certainty that Miss Deborah Walker is innocent of aiding and assisting Lloyd, wife and child to escape.*

But it was such a lie! And she wanted *him* to lie, too. He felt hot anger, and then sorrow that Deborah seemed to have collapsed. He needed time to think.

"I don't have to answer you now," he said.

"Of course not!" Mr. Nicholas stood up. "Think about it, Mr. Bowen. I know of your warm regard for Miss Walker. I'm sure you want no harm to come to her. Our prisons are not exactly hotels, and for a woman . . . It would be tragic if she should be made to waste in prison for a crime she has not committed. Shall I come by tomorrow?"

Josh nodded dumbly.

When the jailer let Nicholas out, Josh lay down on the hard bench. Confused thoughts tumbled through his head. What were Deborah's plans for her defense? To say she had nothing to do with the escape and with him? But how would she explain the fact that people had seen her leave the boardinghouse with him the night the Hawkins were missing; that others had seen them in the hack coming and going; and that they had been arrested riding back together from the river? If she couldn't deny these facts, how would she explain them? By saying he had kidnapped *her* together with the Hawkins family? He smiled at the notion. But suddenly it didn't seem funny. What if she was inventing such a story? Putting all the blame on him while she played the innocent victim of *his* plot!

Calming himself, he began to think she couldn't be capable of such a thing. How could anyone believe it to be a duty to aid slaves to escape and then lie about it? If it is your duty to do what is right, then it is equally your duty to acknowledge it. How could it be right to do it and then not be ready when summoned to admit it?

Suddenly Josh realized that *he* was not admitting what he had done. He hadn't thought it through for himself. He was not denying anything—only refusing to speak. Let them prove their case against him, without his cooperation. But when it came to his trial, they would ask how he pleaded, guilty or not guilty. How could he attack Deborah for what she was doing until he knew what was right for himself to do?

All night he wrestled with the decision facing him. And couldn't make up his mind. Toward dawn, he decided he must see Deborah himself.

When he asked Mr. Nicholas if it could be arranged, the man seemed surprised. Perhaps he expected an easy yes, Josh thought. No man refuses a lady's request, is that it? Mr. Nicholas said it would be difficult, but maybe he could get the sheriff to allow them a private meeting.

The next day Josh's irons were taken off his legs. The jailer led him to a large cell at the far end of a corridor, unlocked the door and said, "Fifteen minutes, no more. And don't try anything!"

Then he was alone with Deborah. She had come toward the door as it opened. She did not put out her hand but smiled warmly. He saw she was handsomely dressed, as always, and looked none the worse for her imprisonment. Her room was much larger than his, with two big windows viewing the yard and a grate for burning coal.

"Josh," she said. "You look awful!"

"I must smell as bad as I look," he said. "They can hardly spare a cup of water for me to drink, much less to wash with."

She put her hands to her cheeks, embarrassed by the contrast in their treatment. "I'm sorry," she said. "They seem to be taking better care of me."

"Well, you have friends in Lexington."

"Yes, Mr. Nicholas has been wonderful. . . . He visits me regularly. And he has gotten me some first-rate lawyers—General Combs, Mr. Shy, and Mr. Johnson."

"Sounds very impressive," he said.

"Who's your lawyer, Josh?"

"I haven't any."

"None! Don't you mean to defend yourself?"

"Against whom? The state or you?"

She flushed and drew back a step.

"Why are you so angry with me?"

"I'm not angry. Bewildered, rather."

"Because I'm asking you to sign that affidavit?"

"What are you trying to do, Deborah?"

"I only want to go on doing what you know I've always done."

"So do I," he said. "But in the name of one principle—freedom—you're sacrificing another."

"What other?"

"Truth."

"I'm afraid I don't see it that way, Josh."

He was silent. She moved away, toward a window, and looked out on the scraggly trees outlined against the prison wall. With her back toward him, she said, "Will you sign the paper?"

"If I do, it'll be a lie."

"And if you don't?"

"You'll go to prison." She had made him say it. And hearing his own voice, he knew he could not let that happen. Not if she wasn't ready to go, not if she wanted him to help her.

She turned around. Her eyes were misting over, he thought, but he couldn't be sure with the light in back of her. "You'll sign it?"

He hesitated. It was hard to speak the words. Then he nodded his head. She walked up to him and put her hand on his arm. "Thank you, Josh. I think I know what this means to you."

He turned, went to the door and knocked. Before

the jailer could open it, she said softly, "Josh, maybe you'll be hearing more things about me you won't like. Don't hate me."

The door opened, and he went out.

Two weeks later Deborah was brought to trial. The state had intended to try them together, but her lawyers had succeeded in obtaining a severance of the cases. In the days preceding the trial one of the newspapers carried stories that were obviously intended to win public sentiment for her. Passages from letters she had written from her cell were quoted. In one, sent to a Vermont minister, she had said:

> *I tell my accusers that I defy them; all-powerful as they are, to find an individual in the state, old or young, black or white, bond or free, that will prove that he has, or ever had, the remotest grounds for even suspecting me to be an abolitionist.*
>
> *I deny being what some people say I am, an abolitionist agent, sent on by the New England abolition societies for the purpose of rendering the black population uneasy and discontented, and for aiding and assisting them to elope from bondage.*
>
> *All anyone could ever hold against me is that on one occasion (perhaps when overexcited)*

I remarked in company that if all the black pop-ulation could be banished from our loved country, I would cheerfully go myself to the wild and desert shores of Africa to teach them that they have immortal souls. This was, perhaps, an imprudent remark. If so, pardon me. It is the only one I am guilty of.

Her own father, she said in another letter, was against abolition, and everyone in Vermont knew it. She had never been raised to support the antislavery cause. She never read abolitionist literature, she went on, and she was "as bitterly opposed to what is termed 'Negro-stealing' as Kentuckians them-selves."

Josh's heart turned cold when he read these stories in the paper. He knew now what Deborah had meant when she asked him not to hate her.

The day the trial began the courthouse was filled with angry slaveholders long before Judge Buckner gaveled for order. Deborah pleaded not guilty. Her lawyers made a vigorous fight for five days, trying their best to present her as what they honestly be-lieved her to be—the innocent dupe Josh had used as a cover for his own purpose. His affidavit was read to the jury. Then Deborah testified that he had invited her to attend the wedding in Ohio of his

Kentucky friends, a Mr. George Allen and a Miss Emma Smith, and it was these two, she believed, with their servant boy, who had got into the hack with them. She said the couple had been married by the Reverend John Rankin when they reached Ripley. Several witnesses testified that they had seen the hack and swore all the adult passengers were white.

Late one afternoon, as he brought Josh his supper, the jailer told him that Deborah's case had just gone to the jury. I don't care what happens to her, Josh told himself. But he woke in the dark and found he couldn't sleep for worrying. There was no news in the morning. When the noon meal came, he heard the verdict from the jailer.

"Guilty!"

After all she had done to protect herself? "What was the sentence?" he asked.

"Two years the jury gave her, two years in the pen at Frankfort." The jailer spat a long jet of tobacco juice on the cell floor. "But don't worry," he said sarcastically, "she won't serve much of it."

"How do you know?"

"Too many powerful folks working for her. Why, that damn jury—soon as they handed in the verdict all twelve of them signed a letter to the governor asking him to give her a pardon. Now! Before she's even served a day!"

Some sort of deal must have been made. The jury had to convict because too many Kentuckians, like the jailer, hated abolition and demanded a victim. But the way was already prepared for Deborah to get off lightly. What of himself? The press and her lawyers had painted him as a fanatic who had coldly deceived an innocent girl. He had no chance to be acquitted. There never had been a chance. Evidence or no evidence, this slaveholder's state would manufacture a case against him. And the truth was, by their lights he *was* guilty. . . .

The day of his trial he was taken in chains to the courthouse. He would have no lawyer, he told the court.

"But you must," the judge said, "to protect your rights." And he appointed Samuel Shy, who had been one of Deborah's counselors. There was a whispered conference between the two. Mr. Shy wanted to ask for a postponement so he could prepare Josh's defense.

"No," said Josh. "I know what I want to do. And I can do it right now." The lawyer shrugged. The trial proceeded.

"Joshua Bowen, you are charged under Ken-

tucky statute with enticing slaves to leave their owners and to escape to parts out of this Commonwealth."
And then the three indictments were read out against
him. That he, Joshua Bowen, "having no lawful
claim or color of title to the said slaves, Lloyd,
Harriet and Joe Hawkins, did aid, abet and assist
them in leaving their said owners and in escaping
to parts beyond the limits of this Commonwealth, to
wit, the state of Ohio."

"Joshua Bowen, how do you plead, guilty or not
guilty?"

"I plead guilty."

Uproar in the crowded courtroom. His Honor,
Judge Buckner, gaveled furiously for order. No one
had expected this. They had settled themselves for
a grand treat—the state's attorney forcing this lying
abolitionist to the wall—and now the defendant had
admitted his guilt!

"Do you throw yourself upon the mercy of the
court, then?"

"I do, Your Honor. But I ask the court to permit
me to speak to the jury on my own behalf."

"You may proceed, Mr. Bowen."

Josh walked to the jury box, moving painfully
because the leg irons had rubbed his skin raw and
his muscles were weak from disuse. He turned a
chair around, leaning with his hands on its back.

The twelve men were all eying him curiously. He felt they had not really seen him—Josh Bowen— until now, but rather some mythical monster, practicing every deception to undermine and destroy the institution they all lived by. He began without polite preliminaries.

"I am an abolitionist by upbringing," he said, speaking slowly, in a quiet voice. "If I had been born and educated here, I might have been as you are. But I was raised to regard slavery as a sin. I believe that to relieve men from slavery is a virtue, not a crime.

"What is a slave?" He let the question linger in the air, waiting so long for them to think about it that a few began to fidget or clear their throats.

"I think a slave is a person held as property, by legalized force, against natural right. In Kentucky the law puts the armed force of sheriffs, police and state militia at the disposal of the man who holds his fellow man as a slave. The public force of the community backs the private force of the individual slaveholder.

"But how can the law make a man property, when man is not by nature a slave? What would you think if the Kentucky legislature were to propose a law to make men into sausages? You smile at the proposition. If any of you believed the legislature meant to do it, you would think it the worst thing the legislature had ever done. But can you tell me that to make a man into a sausage would be worse than to make him into a slave? The one is just as sensible a proposition as the other.

"No, a man is free, free by the law of the Creator, which endows every human being with the inalienable right to freedom. God's law cannot be repealed by an inferior law which asserts that man is property. You may enforce such an inferior law by chains and guns and gallows. But every man your law holds to be a slave *continues* to be a man, nevertheless. And as a man, he has the inalienable right to freedom. As his fellow man, I have the duty to guarantee his freedom and to liberate him from the bonds another man may put him in."

There were scattered cries of "Nigger-stealer! Nigger-stealer!" from the crowd. The judge banged his gavel.

Josh turned to the spectators. "I do not deny what I have done. I helped a man, a woman and a child to find their way to freedom. That act may make me guilty under the law of Kentucky. So be it. But I have not broken the law of humanity."

He stood straight now, in front of the jury. "Your legislature cannot authorize injustice by law. It cannot take away the securities of life and liberty. It cannot repeal the laws of Nature. It cannot oblige me to do wrong or neglect my duty. Nor is any court bound to enforce such unjust law. On the contrary, the court honors justice if it refuses to enforce such a law.

"I hope, then, that this court will rule in favor of liberty. But whatever decision is made here must be judged too at the tribunal of public opinion— the opinion not only of the people of Kentucky, not only of the people of America, but of the whole world.

"I most earnestly pray that the judgment of the court in this case may earn the respect of all men everywhere who love liberty and justice."

With this, he walked back to the prisoner's place and sat down.

The courtroom was silent for a moment. Then angry buzzing began. What kind of court was this to let such vicious speeches be made? Looking out over the rows of benches, Josh could not find a friendly face. He had changed nobody's mind.

The jury filed out. In less than half an hour it was back. It found the defendant guilty and sentenced him to five years at hard labor on each of the three indictments.

Fifteen years . . .

14

They Never Saw the Sky

The day after he was sentenced Josh was taken from Megowan's jail, secured in heavy iron fetters and driven to the penitentiary at Frankfort. As he came up to the prison the walls blotted out the sky. He went through a gate flanked by tall twin towers. The prison walls looked four feet thick and five times as high as a man. They shut in a few acres on which stood several buildings. Down the long sides of the yard, facing each other, he saw two big double-storied buildings of brick. One contained work-shops, and the other the hemp factory. A small building housed the women.

Josh was taken to the men's cell block. Long and narrow, it rose three tiers high. Again he was thoroughly searched, stripped, every piece of cloth-ing shaken out. Belt, shoelaces, sharp objects—anything a man might use to free himself from the law by suicide or flight—were taken from him. The guards shaved his head and his beard, slapped a woolen cap on him, dressed him in stripes and took him to his cell. Like all the others, it was about four by seven, and seven feet high at the center of its arch. The brick walls were windowless. The floor was of rough planks, with a straw mattress flung in one corner.

The door clanged shut, and he stretched out on the mattress. It was alive with fleas. He was tired; his bones seemed turned to water. A lump grew in his throat, so big it threatened to choke him. He opened his mouth, sighed and took in the foulest air he had ever breathed. His eyes roved the walls and ceiling, dimly seen in the flickering light of the candle stuck in a niche. Once whitewashed, now they were mottled gray and brown and streaked with green. He touched the green. It was slime from the damp. Then he noticed that the walls—almost every inch of them—were scratched with names and messages. Inscriptions everywhere, barely visible at first. BOB WORLEY . . . HENERY WAS HERE . . . ELI THOMAS DON'T FORGET . . . RACHEL! Prisoners before him crying they were alive—even here they were alive.

He had been brought in after the last meal of the day. The prisoners were already locked in their cells. He had seen no one but officers and guards.

"Silence. That's the golden rule here," the officer had said. "Speak only on pain of the lash." Work together by day, isolation at night. A prison system that believed bad company had led men astray: to keep them in separate cells would help them more readily to reform.

He lay still, feeling he was buried in a tomb. Fifteen years! Would every hour be like this? He couldn't live in here. He would die. He couldn't breathe. The air was stifling. He thought of the men all around him, invisible, unknown. But they would know him. Hate him for what he was. Who were they? Where were they? He strained to hear any sound through the silence. Then it came, the soft groans, curses, sighs, the rustle of straw as prisoners turned on their mattresses. Not alone. But forsaken. His own life far away, receding behind wall after wall after wall.

And then a voice calling, it seemed from far away . . .

"Who——are——you? Who——are——you?" It came softly again and again.

He put his ear to the wall, waited. Then it drifted in once more. "Who——are——you?"

"Joshua——Bowen," he answered, imitating the subdued and spaced-out sound.

There was a pause. It stretched out for what

seemed many minutes. Then he understood why. The heavy footfall of the guard, making his periodic round. The light from the guard's lantern pierced the small iron grille high on his cell door, and swept over his ceiling. When the guard had passed, again the voice came:

"What——you——in——for?"

How should he answer? What was the crime?

"Helping——slaves——to run away."

Silence on the other side of the wall.

Josh waited.

"Helping——slaves——to run off," he tried again.

"Done heard you the first time, you bastard!" said the faint voice.

He fell back on his straw. The hours dragged by. Gradually a numbness stole over him, pulled him down and under. He slept.

At daylight the first bell rang. Those first mornings the harsh sound exploded in his head, and he awoke in a confusion of dark and noise, not knowing where he was. All too soon the scuffling sounds from the nearby cells, the coughing and spitting, told him he was here. He got up and dressed. A second bell rang and the cell doors opened. They stood at attention at their doors, absolutely silent. At the third bell they tramped heavily in formation to their place of labor. There they washed themselves rapidly (there were no baths, either warm or cold—only basins and buckets) and got to work at once.

He was set to sawing stone. At the other end of the saw they put a man about his own size. Copper colored, he had big hands and a thick shock of hair combed to the side, revealing a scar that might have come from a burn. "Your partner," said the guard, nodding toward the man. "Try stealing this nigger!" Isaac Edwards barely glanced at him. They got to work in silence. Only what few words were needed to get on with the job were permitted. If anyone passed, official or visitor, they could not talk to him, even look at him.

At mealtime, a first bell rang to tell them to get ready.

At the second bell each shop formed a double line, the foreman in the rear, and marched to the eating shed in silence. They stood by their places until the table bell rang, the signal for them to sit down. Cold bread and bacon was dumped on his iron plate. Ten minutes to eat, in silence. The bread was of the coarsest corn meal, made with water only and baked stone-hard. It was moldy, but if he left even the smallest crust, he would be whipped for it. The bacon stank. A hog would have trouble downing it. The coffee was made of burnt rye in a forty-pail kettle, with the same grounds cooked over and over for weeks. Molasses sweetened the evening meal, and sometimes there would be soup, potatoes, or green corn, if they did not cost too much.

When a man wanted bread, he held his hand up; when meat, his knife; when soup, his spoon. If he made a sign, and it was not noticed, he rattled the utensil on the table, then held it up again.

When the table bell rang the second time, all rose at the same moment and marched back to their work in the same order as they came.

As the day's work ended, the night bell rang, and they prepared to leave. At the second ringing, they plodded back to their cells. Down the long corridor, high on an outer wall, Josh saw the cell block's lone window; it let in a faint glimmering light and some air. Each man passing under it would slow his step and lift his head to it, reaching for a healing ray of light.

Lamps and candles burned all the time, even at midday, to give them some light by which to do their chores. From their cells they never saw the sky. They lived in flickering darkness.

When the prisoners reached their cells, they stood in silence by their doors while the roll was called. Then the guard signaled, and they disappeared into their holes.

ALL CONVERSATION IN THE CELLS IS
PARTICULARLY FORBIDDEN.

Silence.

Everywhere.

All the time.

The nights were the worst. The only sounds were
the tread of the guard when he made his rounds, a
scratching on the wall by rat or prisoner, the hoarse
rattle of a sick man struggling to breathe, a sharp
cry from someone far off lost in a dream. He had
heard nothing from anyone outside—the Coffins, his
parents (did they know?), friends. Was he forgotten
already?

No matter how he pushed it away, the thought
of FIFTEEN YEARS came back again and again.

If he could break it down, maybe he could find
a way to live with it. He begged the loan of the
foreman's slate, scratched feverishly at the figures:

$$365 \times 15 = 5,475 \text{ days}$$
$$5,475 \times 24 = 131,400 \text{ hours}$$
$$131,400 \times 60 = 7,884,000 \text{ minutes}$$
$$7,884,000 \times 60 = 473,040,000 \text{ seconds}$$

The numbers gripped his mind, would not let
go. Anguish welled up in him. It was a cold lump
of iron in his chest that he could not get rid of. At
first the only thing that could distract him was physical discomfort. By the end of the first week he

noticed he would start shivering almost as soon as the cell door closed on him in the evening. The cell block was in the center of the prison yard, right where the ground was depressed. No proper foundation had been laid when they built the prison long ago. After every storm the rain flooded in and made a bed of mud beneath the cells. To make it worse, the roof always needed repair. There was only one iron stove in the corridor to ease the chill. But it could never make him feel dry enough or warm enough.

On the ground floor, where he was, the cells had two ventilating passages, but they went only into the attic and were of little use in dispelling the stink. The two tiers above, which needed even more air, had only one ventilator, equally useless. When the prison's outer door was closed at night, whether in summer or winter, breathing was like swallowing filth. He had nightmares of drowning in a cesspool.

Six weeks after he began serving his sentence, Josh was summoned by the keeper, Captain Newton Craig. When he was awaiting trial, Craig had boasted that once he had Joshua Bowen in his prison, he would flog him till he disclosed every last thing he knew about running off slaves. But strangely, Craig had paid no attention to Josh. He seemed to have forgotten his threats.

"Bowen," he said, "I have good news." For him? What could it be? "The governor has pardoned Deborah Walker."

So soon!

"Didn't expect that, eh? Well, it's true, it's true! She left here yesterday. Must be in Cincinnati by now. Took quite an effort, but we managed it all right."

"Managed it?" said Josh.

"Her friends, of course. Starting with the best people in Lexington—loyal, they are, never desert a friend. Didn't take long for them to get the state capital behind them. Why nearly every man jack of the legislature signed a petition for her pardon."

"And the governor went along."

"Certainly. Asked my advice, first, he did. How does Miss Walker behave in prison, he wanted to know. Like the true gentlewoman she is, said I. Never gave me a moment's trouble. Took her out of that cell many an evening, I did, so she could sit with me and my wife. A fine talker she is, too! Enjoyed our conversations. A pity the jury had to go against the evidence of their own eyes and convict her. But that's politics. Anyhow, they all knew she'd have to be pardoned right soon."

"I'm pleased for her sake, Captain."

"You ought to be! Got her into trouble in the first place, you did!"

Josh was silent.

"You're a clever young fellow, Bowen. I can see why Miss Walker took a liking to you. But if you don't learn something in here, you won't be worth a damn to yourself or anyone else."

"What do you mean?"

"*Sir!*"

"What do you mean, sir?"

"I mean you're a lot smarter than the white trash I got in here. Those fellas are good for damn little. Most of them nothing but burglars, horse thieves, counterfeiters, rapists, murderers. But here you come, a Yankee with some learning, and you do something real evil—stealing niggers. Why, man, down here that's the worst crime a white man can commit— take another man's property and run it off! You plain lucky that Lexington mob didn't string you up."

"I sure am," said Josh.

"Now you know it." The captain rose, walked around to the front of his desk and sat on the edge. "Sit down, boy," he said, motioning to a bench.

The captain's voice became earnestly confidential. "You too smart to keep doing what you been doing all along. Jury gave you only fifteen years.

Could have been sixty. Miss Walker, she told me you not a hardened abolitionist. Just a boy loose from home, with wild ideas about saving the world. It's the preacher in you, she says. Took all that Bible stuff too hard. But no reason why you can't get over it. So I'm telling you, if you behave right in here, and forget all that abolition foolishness, maybe you'll get out before your term is up. Maybe, I say, maybe. You got to prove first you a different man."

"Captain," he said, "can I ask you a question?"

"Shoot, boy."

"I know the prisoners are allowed mail once a month. But I haven't been given any yet."

"You right, Bowen. Mail once a month. But it's my policy to see how a new man behaves first. You been getting some mail, but I been holding it."

"Can I see it now?"

Craig unlocked a cabinet in the corner, fumbled through a mound of paper and took out a thin packet of letters. Josh reached for it, but the captain shook his head. "Wait a minute now," he said. He held up the letters one by one. Josh could see the seals were broken. They had all been opened. "Two from Levi Coffin . . . we don't allow no abolition nonsense in here. And this one's from that crazy man, Garrison. You don't get that neither. Here are two you can have. From your father."

Josh took them, trembling in his eagerness. "You can read them now," Craig said. Josh went over to a window and unfolded one.

At the sight of the stiff, angular writing his heart began to pound so hard he thought Craig must hear it.

Son,

We learned where you are in the newspaper. It told about your trial and sentence. Also a letter from friends in Ohio, telling why you got into trouble. Your mother cried so she could not write. So I am. What is innocent or guilty? It is hard to tell now. But mother says no matter what you did, she knows you did it out of love. We will try to get them to free you. But I don't know how yet.

Father

He read the letter a second time, rapidly, and put it in his pocket. So they knew, the Coffins knew, everyone knew. His heart felt infinitely lighter. He had not been forgotten.

Captain Craig said, "There was five dollars in

that letter. I've entered it on your account. You can draw on it at the commissary."

As he started to open the other letter, he saw that Craig was watching him closely. It was only a few lines:

> *Your mother died three days ago at five in the morning. Her heart gave out suddenly in her sleep. We buried her today. Bear up, son. She would have said it is God's will.*
>
> *Father*

He looked up at the keeper. The letter was weeks old. The man had known the news in it this long and had said nothing. Josh's eyes filled with tears.

"I'm sorry, boy," said the captain. He went to take Josh's arm. But he shook him off and turned to the door. A guard took him back to the stone-cutting shop. As soon as the foreman's back was turned, Isaac whispered, "What Craig want?"

"For me to be a good boy. No more slave-stealing . . ."

Isaac grinned at him. If he could only tell Isaac about his mother. But he needed time to get used to it, to the knowledge that he had not seen her for so long, and now he never would again. It was bad enough for him; what would his father—a man locked tight in himself—do with her gone? The warmth had come all from her, like a good fire keeping a house livable. It was out now, and his father would face a long winter alone.

Josh could talk now, in spite of the rule of silence. He had soon learned what all the others had: how to carry on a conversation with only the slightest movement of the lips. Once that was mastered, the tide of information rolled in. From Isaac Edwards he had found out about the blacks in prison. There were only a small number, most of them kept apart. "None of us be slaves," said Isaac. "We all free, cept they slap us in the pen cause we do the baddest things." Josh knew the slaveholders themselves punished their own blacks and had their own jails. It was the free blacks who were tried in the public courts and sentenced to the penitentiary. Josh got news and he gave it. Who was just in, who was getting out, who was sick, who spied, who flattered, who betrayed, who'd been beaten.

Almost everyone nursed the good will of the guards. If just one was down on you, it was enough to make life an even worse hell. Disobey, or have him say you did, and the punishment was to be flung into the hole—a solitary dark cell, day and night without light or sound. Or take the lash. The rules said no more than forty-eight hours in the hole on the same offense at any one time, or ten lashes. But men with absolute power paid little attention to the rules.

One of the things Josh found it hardest to get used to was that while they forced him to live alone so much, the rest of the time they treated him like an animal caged in a zoo. Visitors were allowed into the prison solely out of idle curiosity. Not family or friends; they were denied visits. But total strangers, who strolled about the yard, lingered in the workshops, gaped at the men, made any remarks they liked, from pious homily to vicious insult. While the convicts were compelled to silence. He wondered, was it the state's belief that putting its criminals on display would keep the others honest?

The day-to-day life was the round of work. The stone-cutting was hard. The poor food, the stifling air, the restless nights, the deadly monotony—they wore Josh down badly. He soon lost almost thirty pounds. Craig noticed it and offered a change. Pick what shop you like, he said. Josh asked for shoemaking. It was a craft, and he enjoyed learning it. There was the satisfaction of doing something useful and doing it as well as he could.

Now and then there was a letter from his father. News of the farm, the neighbors (names he had almost forgotten), and always a line to let him know he was trying to have him set free. But how, he never said. It was so vague he began to believe his father could do nothing and was only trying to keep his spirits up. He was allowed to write him—and no one else—only once a month. He did it without fail, but the captain, who read all his letters, made clear he could say very little: only the prison routine (never any criticism of it) or a remembered moment of life back home in the old days. One became too dull to describe and the other too painful to recall. He could not bring himself to write about his mother.

Gradually he stopped adding up the time he had yet to serve. The edges of his mind blurred. He drifted along from one day to the next, carried to some unknown destination.

15

Money Is My Religion

The day Zebulon Ward took the keys of the prison, Josh's sleep was shattered. The new keeper called all the prisoners to the chapel. For weeks there had been rumors that Captain Craig was on the way out. The keeper got his position under a lease system. He bought it from the state for a four-year term. Craig's term was ending, and the new man, Ward, had bid higher, offering Kentucky $6000 a year.

Ward stepped up to the pulpit and took off his coat. He was a tall middle-aged man who walked like an ex-West Pointer. A broad beard spread over his face, helping to conceal the pockmarks that cratered it.

"Men," he said, "you are not going to like me. But I don't like you either, and we hardly been introduced." He laughed, a hoarse noise that sounded like grating wheels.

"I came here to make money. Captain Craig

made money out of this lease too. But I'm going to make *more* money, and I'm going to do it if I kill you all.

"Some of you won't like the hours of work I'm setting. But I tell you, I will let no man set the clock on me. If any of you want to claim the ten-hour limit on your time of working, just get right up and go to your cells."

They all sat still.

Ward waited a moment. "All right, I'm a man of few words and prompt action. Do your duties, or I'll make you!"

The words fell like blows.

The next day, Josh was summoned to see the keeper.

"Bowen," he said, "you know my reputation?"

"Yes, sir, I do." The prison grapevine had already carried the report that back in Covington they called Zeb Ward the Bloodsucker.

"Money's my religion. And this prison is the best place I've had yet to practice it. I know about you, Bowen. You're a religious man too. Only stealing niggers is your religion. I mean to convert you to my brand. Craig's been letting you get away with murder in that shoe shop. You need a wee bit more discipline. I'm putting you on hemp. Now get out!"

Hemp. Josh sagged when he heard the word.

He had been lucky to escape it up to now. Hemp was the biggest money crop for Kentucky's planters. And the biggest money-maker for the wardens. Four out of five of the prisoners worked on it, making rope and bagging out of the tough fiber. Every dollar the warden could squeeze out of prison labor above expenses and the price of his lease was profit for his own pocket.

The guard turned him over to the hemp boss. Jack Page ruled his little kingdom from an office tucked into the ground floor of one of the workshops. "Let's see, you been here six months, Bowen, and you still alive." He shook his head sadly. "Abolitionists is stubborn devils. Hanging you all would be cheaper for the state. I hear Mr. Ward wants you to learn this business from the ground up. Maybe you two aim to go partners when you both through here?" He laughed. It broke the geometric pattern of his face—the dark horizontal burn of the eyebrows, the long slash of the mouth, the vertical plunge of the nose. A meticulous man, Josh thought, and very sure of himself.

"But he'll have to wait for a bit, won't he? Let's see now"—and again he consulted his record book—"something like fourteen-and-a-half years to go? Well"—slamming the book shut—"that'll give us plenty of time to teach you the trade.

"Now here's how we'll do it. You'll start in the hackling house. Next we'll give you a turn at spinning. And then a taste of the weaving. That way we'll see what you do best in. Mind you, we expect you to do your best at everything." He nodded toward a rack on the wall. It held several cats—long ropes of many strands with a big knot tied at the end of each. "Home product," he said. "Make them right here. They'll help you try harder."

Page paused. "Think you'll like it?"

"I guess I'll have to."

"A sensible boy!" He took Josh's arm and steered him to the door. Opening it, he said, "Just don't give me any trouble. I won't like it."

The hackling house was where the hemp was dressed at steel-toothed hackles after being broken from the stalk. The room was so full of dust that on a still, dry day it was hard to distinguish a man from a block of wood. A crew of twenty-four did the hackling, and in one week Josh saw six of them taken to the prison hospital, their lungs so choked with dust they could not breathe. In another week four of them were dead. By the end of the month he was coughing and spitting all day, and waking in the night, terrified that he would drown in his own phlegm.

Now Page sent him to the spinning room. The

foreman looped around him a belt, with an eight-inch string attached, to which was fastened a stick with a notch, called a drag. This was hitched to a rope running on pulleys at each end. The ropes turned the wheels, so that the faster Josh moved backwards, the faster the wheel turned, with the dust rising right under his nose and inhaled at every breath. The thread of the warp, twice the thickness of wrapping twine, could cut through the skin. The filling was sometimes thick with little hemp sticks, which could rip clear to the bone of the spinner's hand. Soon his hands were like raw meat. They had only begun to toughen when it was time to switch again.

Weaving he found not as dusty as spinning or hackling. But it was physically much more wearing. Before Ward came, the common task at weaving was 150 yards a day. Ward demanded 208. Page broke down the task by the hour, so that the foreman could keep constant check on each prisoner's production.

Two hundred and eight yards—37,440 shots of the shuttle by hand. From daybreak to dark the weavers sweated, knowing whoever was behind would feel the whip. Every day came the slash of the cat, and often two were whistling through the air at the same time, the howling of the victims echoing off the walls. No matter how hard he tried, Josh could not make more than 165 yards of that bagging. In Captain Craig's time, that would have been more than enough. But it wouldn't do for Zebulon Ward. At any moment of the day Josh was liable to hear his name yelled out.

"Bowen! Come down here!"

It could be first thing in the morning, or just before noon, or after noon, or last thing in the evening. Off came his shirt and down came his pants. A sign from Page, and two of the guards, both well-whiskied, would peel down to the waist for their work. The rope cut deep into his bare back and bottom nearly every stroke. He felt each lash clear through to his lungs. First Ed laid on, until he tired; then he would hand the cat to Rufe. Sometimes it was thirty-nine stripes, sometimes twice that, and if it went higher, he often passed out. Ten feet away the walls were spattered with particles of flesh and blood.

If he was conscious, it was back to his place to weave. Sitting down was an agony. It was like sitting on boils. The guards let him borrow a blanket or take his coat, roll it up small and sit on it like a saddle.

The bad food, his congested lungs and the beatings were destroying him. He was behind in his work regularly. One morning, ordered by Jack Page to carry eight reels of hempen yarn upstairs, he staggered under the load and let a reel fall.

"Worn yourself out stealing niggers?" Page said. "I'll teach you what honest work is." He stripped Josh down and flogged him himself.

Repeatedly Josh asked permission to see the keeper. "I can't make the task," he said. "I'll never be able to make it. Let me talk to Mr. Ward." Page ignored his requests. "I know you can't," he said. "*I don't want you to*. . . . Now don't stand there like a fool. Get a move on!"

Three more months dragged by. He had hoped to be sent back to hackling or spinning. Certainly he had done better in those shops. But Page showed no interest in a change. Then one day a committee from the legislature descended on the prison for annual inspection. It was the members' duty to look into and correct conditions, if necessary. They divided up, so that each shop could be visited in the course of the day. Josh was at his weaving when the keeper came around, escorting a military-looking man with a benevolent shock of white hair. They stopped at his bench.

"Is this the notorious prisoner?" the stranger asked, smiling.

"Yes, Colonel, this is Bowen. The slave-stealer."

"I read about you in the papers, Bowen. I was

in New Orleans when they tried you. How does he behave, Mr. Ward?"

"Well enough, Colonel."

"Too bad he didn't behave outside. Now, if you'll excuse us, Mr. Ward, I'd like to talk to the prisoner alone." The keeper walked away.

"Tell me, Bowen, how does Mr. Ward treat the prisoners?"

"Sir, I am a prisoner."

"I know you are! What I want to know is how the prison is conducted. Are you treated well?"

Josh could feel Ward's eyes burning into him from the far side of the room.

Again, "Sir, I am a prisoner."

The colonel bit his lip, looked from Josh to Ward and back again. Then he slapped his cane against his leg and went over to Ward. They left the room.

The next day Josh was taken to Ward's office.

"Bowen, what in hell did you say to the colonel yesterday?"

"Nothing, sir."

"You're a liar! I could see that you said something."

"The something said was nothing."

"Don't give me any riddles! *What* did you say?"

"I said, 'I am a prisoner.' That's all."

"Only that! And you call that nothing? That was

like telling him straight out you are not treated right in here!"

"Am I, sir?"

"You son of a bitch! Are you treated any different from the others?"

"Perhaps not. Only a little more of the same."

"Then why did you give the colonel the impression that you are abused?"

"Because I am. We all are. Worked till we're crippled or killed and flogged if we can't keep up."

"You're lying again. I've had no complaints from the other prisoners."

"How could you? The foremen and the guards never let us come to see you. I'm sure they don't tell you what goes on in the shops. You'd rather not know."

"Bowen, you more than a nigger-stealer. You more rotten than that. You need a chance to think things over. Guard!"

The man came in. "Mr. McDowell, the hole for this prisoner. Three days."

The guard led him through the corridors and down a long flight of stairs. At the bottom, the guard lifted a heavy iron lid. A stink like a sewer flooded up. He grabbed Josh from behind and shoved him down. Josh fell into a pit. The lid clanked down over his head, a chain rattled into place, a lock turned.

Total blackness.

16

A Buried Life

The dark was more than absence of light. Chill fog that crept into ears, nose, mouth, eyes, pierced clothes, sank into bones, turned blood into ice. He lay huddled on the dirt floor until his sluggish brain warned him he might freeze to death. He stood up slowly, held out his arms, trying to feel how big the hole was. A tentative step in any direction and he could touch the earthen walls. A hole, a pit dug into the bottom of the cell house. Faint scrambling of small feet, and then the persistent sound of gnawing. Rats. He shuddered violently, shrank back to the wall, recoiled from its clammy touch. The rats— inside the hole, or burrowing on the outside?

Slowly his eyes adjusted to the dark. He could see the walls dimly, and above his head, out of reach, the iron lid shutting him in. Time passed without measure. Minutes? hours? He could no longer tell. He sank into a half-sleep, starting awake when the gnawing seemed to grow louder and the dread of vicious teeth made his muscles tense agonizingly. He prayed for the sound of a human voice. Only the slow drip of water, the frightful gnawing. He yelled. No answer. He began talking, filling the void with his own voice, telling himself stories, repeating old conversations, inventing exchanges with Jacob Axley, with Sam, with his father, Levi, Deborah. When he heard himself babbling, he stopped. Scenes from the past surfaced, and he drifted away on them. Hunger. How long was it since he had eaten? Were they letting him go without food for the whole three days? Surely that much time had passed.

A rattle of chains above, the key turning in the lock, the lid slowly rising. Light slashed into the hole, blinding him. When he could see, it was McDowell's face peering over the edge. Silently a hand stretched down with a lump of bread and a cup of water. He reached for them, gulping the air greedily.

"Mr. McDowell, you letting me out now?"

"In a hurry, Bowen? You ain't been in hardly one day!"

The lid slammed down. He sank to the floor. One day, only *one* day! He put the bread to his mouth and started to gnaw.

———————

His own cell was like home after the hole. Its cold, its wetness, its stink—they were nothing to him when he could stretch out on the straw under a blanket, watch the candle keeping off the dark, eat three times a day, and hear the living sounds of men. He was too weak to work. Zeb Ward knew he would be and let him stay in his cell a few days until his body began to recover strength enough for him to return to the weaving shop.

Time was again marked off by the rhythm of the bells. The routine of each day, repeated forever, made existence automatic. The weeks melted into months and the months into seasons. The heat of summer, the cold of winter, the dullness of Sundays, a departure, an arrival, nothing changed the mechanical rhythm of this buried life.

His work was as hard as ever, but Jack Page no longer demanded the impossible. For a while Josh had brought excitement into Page's gray life, nearly as monotonous as the prisoners'. But now the "nigger-stealer" had sunk to the bottom of Page's mind and was lost there among the anonymous striped machines fixed to the shuttles of his shop.

Denied visitors, denied newspapers, denied mail from anyone but his family, denied talk with his fellow prisoners, Josh slid into a private world. He fed off his own fantasies. There was nothing else to stimulate him inside these walls. The prison gossip that stole past the alert guards became only trivia. It was impossible to discuss ideas. What was worse, he realized he no longer even cared to. He had lost that desire together with the will to make decisions. Prison left him no decisions to make. That had been the hardest thing to get used to. In between the depressions that seized him he would sometimes wonder what he would do with the years of his sentence if he could live them outside. At first he knew he would be doing exactly what had brought him within these walls. But as time passed the ties between himself and life outside seemed to stretch to the breaking point. When he heard from no one it became easy to think it was their fault. He had become invisible to them. They did not believe in his existence. Anger against the slave system turned into anger against his friends. He felt forgotten, forsaken.

Spring came early his third year in prison. The warmth coaxed the buds open on the two stunted trees in the yard. Marching to meals, they all moved with a lighter step, lifting their eyes to the clean blue of a sky speckled with soft white clouds.

In April he sat through his third birthday in a prison cell. Now he was twenty-three. And half the number of years he had already lived stretched before him to be killed within these stone walls. How long would twelve years more be? He would lie awake for hours measuring the passage of that much time. From birth to twelve? From twelve to now? From five to seventeen, when he had left the farm in Pike? He remembered summers in childhood when time stood still. A day, an afternoon—sometimes they lasted forever. Now it was easy to believe he was always happy then.

When he let himself think of the years still to be dragged out, there was no horizon to time. He began to think he would go crazy if he did not find something to occupy his mind.

One day he asked to see Zeb Ward.

"Bowen," the keeper said, "you been so good I forgot about you. Takes just a little taste of the hole to make a man behave. Now ain't that right?"

"Maybe so, Mr. Ward."

"What you want?"

"I'd like to start a Sunday school."

"*You?* In *here?*" It was the second time Josh had heard the keeper laugh. It came out in short, convulsive snorts.

"Why not? I know the prison is supposed to provide a minister to preach a sermon to the men each Sabbath."

"Who told you that, boy? Jailhouse lawyer?"

"Everyone says so."

"How you hear anything when you men ain't allowed to talk?" But he smiled. Ward knew the rule couldn't be rigidly enforced. If it were, the prisoners would go mad.

"And besides," said Josh, "the prisoners are supposed to get classes in reading, writing and arithmetic. They need instruction and encouragement."

"You offering to take that on, too?"

"I'm a licensed preacher, and I can teach the three Rs better than most in here."

"You still cocky, boy. Too cocky for a man with twelve years in front."

Josh said nothing. The keeper tilted his chair back and propped up his feet on his desk. "You a convict, Bowen, and an abolitionist too. What folks say when they hear I got a convict and a nigger-stealer preaching and teaching to my boys?"

"They'll say two things, Mr. Ward. They'll say the keeper's doing his duty, giving the men what the law says they're supposed to have. And when they learn I'm the one doing it, you can remind them that Paul preached in prison, where they had put him for breaking the law."

Ward puckered up his mouth, squinted hard at Josh and slowly lowered the front legs of his chair to the floor. "I'll be damned, Bowen, if you ain't the smart one. If I let you do what you want, it'll make me look good, eh? But how'll I know you ain't gonna be peddling that abolitionist line to my boys?"

"Mr. Ward, do you ever let two prisoners stay in a room together without a guard around? You may even want to come to Sunday school yourself."

The keeper laughed. "Maybe I will some day, just to see what a Yankee schoolmarm's like."

The keeper told the prisoners that Sunday classes in the three Rs would be open to all except blacks and men under disciplinary punishment. A third of the prisoners were illiterate. Another third could read and write, but very poorly. Yet almost all the prisoners volunteered. Anything to break the monotony.

Josh taught every Sunday, running classes all through the day. The prison had a fund of $250 a year to pay for preaching and teaching expenses. Ward let Josh draw on it for slates, primers, paper and pencils. They were handed out when class began and taken back when it ended. Ward would allow no one to use them in between. "Might smuggle out messages," he said. Guards were always on hand to observe the lessons. Josh used the primers to teach the fundamentals, and made the Bible the meat of history and geography as much as of religion and morality.

But it proved too limited a diet. The men were more interested in today's goings on than in the dusty wars of Nebuchadnezzar. The prison had no library, nor were the men allowed to receive books from the outside. Josh knew Zeb Ward received newspapers every day. He got the keeper to pass them on so that he could use them to teach with.

Now his depression lifted. He could touch the world. When he fingered the inky pages he picked up the current of life once more. Local news of crops and livestock and weather and market prices and politics. He had the men read short items aloud, helping them to learn the meaning of strange words and how to spell them. Ward had little to fear in this—no Southern paper had a kind word to say for abolition. Often the men wanted to talk about what they read. It was their open chance to avoid the rule of silence, and they took it eagerly. The papers were peppered with paragraphs offering short lessons in Southern manners and morals:

FATAL AFFRAY—*A man by the name of Evan Parker, of Hamilton County, was killed a few days ago by Lemuel Harvey, of the same county. The parties met in the public road, where an old quarrel about their lands was renewed—Parker making the attack with a bowie knife, which Harvey wrested from his hand, and in turn inflicted the deadly wound.*

AFFAIR OF HONOR—*A hostile meeting was had between Mr. Thomas Butler King and Mr. Charles Spalding on Monday, the 6th inst. Weapons, pistols—distance, ten paces. Two shots were fired without effect, when on the intervention of friends, the affair was adjusted, and the parties exchanged friendly salutations. The difficulty originated from some circumstances connected with the recent canvass of the two gentlemen while candidates for Congress before the people of this District.*

PAINFUL RUMOR—*There was a painful rumor in Vicksburg, Miss. on the 24th inst., that a difficulty recently occurred between some of the students and professors of the Centenary College in Miss., and that one of the professors was shot. We hope it may not be well founded.*

DUEL—*A duel was lately fought between Mr. Clingman of North Carolina and Mr. Yancy of Alabama, members of the present Congress, a short distance from Bladensburg. Neither of them was hurt. Mr. C's ball struck the vacant air, and Mr. Y's the ground. Honor was satisfied, and the parties shook hands. An ineffectual attempt was made in the House of Representatives to censure the guilty parties.*

Let a dispute develop, Josh thought, and shooting or stabbing seemed the only way to settle it. Rich and poor alike killed a man with whom they quarreled from a sense of duty, much as they would kill a partridge from a sense of pleasure. But the prisoners never saw such stories in that light. Violence was the code they lived by. It was what had put many of them behind bars.

One Sunday, when the keeper was sitting in the back of the class, Josh had a convict read aloud a news item headed "A Negro Killed." Josh had made it appear a casual choice. He wanted to see what the men's reaction would be. The reader, himself serving a long sentence for killing a neighbor over a hog that had strayed onto his patch, stumbled through the story:

A NEGRO KILLED—*A Negro belonging to Mr. Allen Barnes was found dead in the woods in the vicinity of Lexington, with a bullet hole through his head. Previous remarks made by one of the citizens of that place, and his known hostility to the owner of the Negro, with other corroborating circumstances, have caused suspicions to be rested upon him; but he has stated, so we are privately informed, that he shot the Negro very early in the morning, before it was light enough to distinguish clearly one object from another, mistaking his head for a wild turkey.*

When he finished, there was an explosion of laughter.

Josh made no comment, simply went on to another news item. The period ended in a few minutes. When the guards took the men out of the chapel, Ward went up to Josh.

"You didn't laugh over that story about the nigger-killing," he said.

"Was it funny?"

"The boys sure thought so."

"Yes, I heard."

"Bowen, I ain't no fool. Few times I been in here to watch, I see you trying to do more'n teach reading and writing. But it don't bother me none. You think you getting anywhere?"

"I'm sure some of the men can do a little better now."

"That ain't what I'm talking about. You think you changing anybody's mind, putting new ideas in some heads?"

"I wouldn't know, Mr. Ward. We're only trying to learn the three Rs here."

Ward laughed. "You got to say that, boy. But I know better. Only it don't bother me, like I told you. These white boys, you ain't gonna teach them nothing. Besides the three Rs. They poor, dirt poor, most all of them, or they wouldn't be here. Got little or no land, no schooling, damn few even got a trade. And they ain't about to work to get anything, either. Hate work!"

"They work hard enough in prison."

"Sure they do! Know why? The cat! Without that little old cat I'd get nothing from them. It's fear, man. Plain fear. Keep them running scared and you got them where you want them."

"Why should they hate to work?" He thought he knew why, but he wanted to see what Ward believed.

"Cause work's for niggers! Ain't no white man gonna do a lick of work if they's a black man around to do it for him. In here, the white's got no choice. Outside, he has."

"But not that many whites own slaves."

"Course not! Don't make no damn difference! White man has to compete with the black boy. How can he? Slave works for nothing. So whatever the white man can do, nigger does it cheaper."

"Seems to me, Mr. Ward, you're saying the slave system works against both—against white labor as well as black."

"*You* saying that, boy, not me. But I ain't about to argue it with you."

"Then why don't the poor whites see it too?"

"Bowen, whites are better 'n blacks. Always have been, always will be. Don't matter if you rich or poor. It's in the blood. These men in here—they know they not friends with the man who owns lots of slaves. He don't invite them into his home. They don't mingle. Still, *they* white too! They *know* they white. That's one sure thing! Just like the planter! They both have the same privilege—to make the nigger work without working themselves. The poor whites, they *feel* better cause *they* white and the nigger's *black*. You go preaching to them about black and white being equal and, man, you get laughed at, or you get killed."

"You think it will ever be different?"

"Maybe some day the black, he'll disappear."

"How could that happen?"

"White blood and black blood, they can't stand each other. Yet they obliged to live on the same land. This got to end some day. One or the other got to go. The blacks bound to rise up some time. When they do, they'll be wiped out."

"Then who'll do the work?"

The keeper laughed. "I don't worry none about that. Me, I won't be here to see it!"

17

A Sweet Pride

It came without warning. It centered in Lexington at first, starting with sudden explosiveness in an insane asylum and spreading rapidly through the city. It struck down rich and poor, black and white. A violent diarrhea, vomiting, severe pain in the pit of the stomach, an intense thirst. Then, rapidly, cramps of the legs, feet, the muscles of the gut. The skin cold and bluish, turning dry and wrinkled as the body fluids drained away. The face pinched, the eyes sunk deep, the pulse at the wrist imperceptible, the voice reduced to a hoarse whisper.

Cholera.

Thousands fled the city in panic. Day and night, cannon boomed in the streets, fired in the hope that the great noise would shake the air and dispel the death it carried. Bodies in the dozens were flung onto carts and trundled over the cobblestones to the burial grounds, where scores of men worked round the clock digging long trenches to hold double rows of coffins. The victims could not be buried fast enough; their bodies lay for days in sheds hastily thrown up.

The plague raced toward every corner of the state. Within a week the prison was attacked. Two men down at first, then another and another and another. The infirmary was too small to hold them. Zeb Ward swept the machines out of a workshop and improvised a hospital. He demanded doctors of the state but, overburdened by the epidemic outside, none came. Desperate, he asked the healthier prisoners for help. Josh volunteered to nurse. What was the risk? The contagion was everywhere. Who knew where it was incubating? He could catch it from the men sitting next to him at meals, or the men in the weaving room. And if he did? Did it matter? To him, to anyone?

There was no medicine to give. No one knew what could stop the cholera. He could only keep the sick as clean as possible and comfort them. With three other volunteers he watched over them in the glow of the burning lamps. By now there were more than sixty men stricken. He turned them over in their straw, gave them something to drink, kept them covered, forcibly held down the delirious. At first he could not tell who was still alive and who was not. Except for the stale odor they began to give off, the corpses seemed like men asleep. Soon he came to know the difference at a glance. The dead mysteriously had the look of objects, of things stiff and empty. Several times a day the keeper looked in, anxious for a sign the disaster was lessening. Josh could only hold out impotent hands as if to say, "What more can we do?"

A week after he started nursing they brought in Jack Page. He was shriveled already, for he had resisted being taken to the hospital. Perhaps he dreaded the sight of death wholesale, or feared in his weakness to face men he had given countless lashes to.

He lay there amid the defecation and death, himself barely alive, the severe lines of his face crumpled into a thousand wrinkles. Whenever he awoke he would strain to lift his head enough to look around, measuring the living against the dead. Josh could feel those eyes summoning him. Moving closer he thought he saw in that gaze the question many fading eyes asked: Why do you let me die while you go on living? But when he reached Page the man's eyes would slowly close and his gray lips would only murmur, "Die, die." What did he mean?

Four days later Page slipped into a coma. Josh went over to him, took his hands—they were surprisingly smooth and soft—and joined them across the man's chest. Beneath, he thought, he could hear the faint slow sound of the heart running down. In a few hours, he closed Page's eyelids with his fingertips.

Sleeping only in snatches, Josh would wake and wonder who had died. He dragged his aching body down the rows, counting the number who had no need of their beds any more and could be carried off for burial, their straw burned, their place cleared for the next man coming in with shaking limbs and frightened eyes. The dying went more slowly now, for the weaker had already fallen. And then one day it was Isaac, Isaac Edwards, the man he had sawed stone with that first day in prison. He was the only black man down with the sickness. Kept off largely to themselves, the few blacks had been spared the contagion that spread so rapidly among the whites.

He came in weak, sweating, trembling, but on his own feet. "Damn fool wouldn't let the men put him on a stretcher," said Zeb Ward. Isaac looked at Josh. "I come in standin up," he said in a voice already hoarse and cracking, "and I be comin out standin up."

"The Lord'll look after that," said the keeper, "but best put a little faith in him, too," nodding toward Josh. And he left.

Leaning on Josh, Isaac lowered himself painfully

onto the fresh straw ready for him. By nightfall he was dreadfully sick, his thin body wracked by the pitiless course of the plague. He lay silent, never asking for anything, but his eyes spoke his anguish. Then one morning Josh looked in Isaac's eyes and saw a calm clearness. A few hours later he passed the bed again, and this time Isaac greeted him with such a radiant smile he felt himself reborn.

Late that night Josh went out into the prison yard, a liberty Zeb Ward permitted him now and then to relieve him from the nauseating room the prisoners had taken to calling the morgue. He stumbled over a stone before his eyes could get used to the darkness. He could see the two trees dimly through a mist. A cool dew hung upon the grass, worn almost bare by processions of marching feet. He filled his lungs with the damp air, feeling a solid sweetness washing through his body. He went over to a tree and sat down, leaning against the trunk. A mild wind caressed his face, and he nodded into a half-sleep. When he opened his eyes, the wind had brushed the mist away, and now, looking up beyond the prison walls, he could see the stars shining. There was only the breathing of the wind in the night, and once the throttled cry of some far-off owl. In the cool, fresh quiet he thought of flowered fields, rivers, green woods, children playing, women laughing. They are real, he thought with a strange joy. They are alive, they are alive. And getting up after a while, he went back in, whispering the news to himself.

The cholera passed its peak and the toll dropped. Within a week there were less than a dozen patients in the sickroom. The others—dead or, like Isaac, returned to their cells.

Two of the volunteer nurses had died, but Josh and the other man had somehow come through untouched.

"Your luck held up," Zeb Ward said to Josh one afternoon. "I never thought you'd live through it."

"Is that why you took me on?"

"Might be," said Ward.

"The cholera could still get me. We're not quite through with it."

"No," said Ward. "It had its chance, and missed you." He looked speculatively at Josh. "Got a visitor, Bowen. Waiting for you in my office."

Josh's heart pounded. A visitor? But he wasn't allowed any!

"Made an exception this time, boy. Think I can justify it after this," and he waved his arm over the sickroom.

"Who is it?"

"Wait and see," he said.

The keeper led the way. They crossed the yard and entered the cell block. Down the corridor and then, at the door of his office, Ward paused. "I'll let you visit by yourselves," he said. "The guard will be outside. Knock when you're finished. Half an hour—that'll be enough." He nodded to the guard and walked away. The guard unlocked the door, and Josh entered the room. At first he couldn't see anyone. The late afternoon sun leveling through the windows was in his eyes. Then from the corner behind him, he heard the voice.

"Josh?" Half-asking, half-saying. And he knew it was his father. He turned. His father came to him, his arms down by his sides but the fingers outstretched, his body as uncertain as his voice. But there was no doubt in Josh. He held out his arms and hugged his father. They stood there a moment. Then, taking his father's arm, Josh led him to a window. They stepped back from each other at the same time, each to search the other's face.

"You don't look so bad, Josh," his father said. "Chest filled out more. Arms thicker, too." Unconsciously Josh ran his hand over his close-cropped head. "Yes," his father said, smiling, "even with the bramblebush gone, I'd have known you on the street, all right. Sometimes I had dreams of you looking like a skeleton."

His father hadn't done well. He could see that. The tall frame he remembered as so erect and powerful was bent now and wasted, the eyes sunk in shadow, the cheeks furrowed deep.

"How are things with you, Pa?"

"The same, much the same. The farm's not doing bad, though I've had to sell a big piece of acreage. More neighbors now. Pike's grown somewhat since you left. But I told you that in my letters." His voice was different too; there was a faint crack in it.

"How did they come to let you see me?"

"I've been trying for a long time, Josh. I knew the rules said no, especially for someone who committed your—who did what you did. But I kept at it. I figured I'd have to show that a lot of people besides your father wanted to help you. I wrote out a petition."

"A petition?"

"Yes, a petition to the governor of Kentucky, asking him to free you now. I started asking all the neighbors to sign it. Wasn't easy. 'A crime's a crime,' some said. 'We got nothing against you, Bowen, but if your boy did wrong, he has to take his medicine like the rest of them.' "

His father paused. Josh could picture those exchanges—his father stopping people in the village store, out on a pasture, behind the pews on Sunday mornings.

"To tell you the truth, Josh, I didn't know what to say the first time someone said that to me. I just said thank you anyway, and went on to someone else. But I kept hearing it. Not from all, but enough to worry me. Pike's small enough as it is, but if I couldn't get our own home folks to sign, how would it go outside?"

He turned to look out the window.

"It brought me to a dead stop, Josh. I'd just sit nights, looking at the fire, trying to find answers in it. I was troubled by the idea the neighbors might be right. Was I asking something for you that it wasn't right to ask for anyone?"

"Let's sit down, Pa," Josh said. They took two of the armchairs and faced them so they could still see the yard. A file of prisoners with their guards trudged by, returning from the workshop to their cells. His father stared hard at them, as though he might know one of the faces. They disappeared around a corner.

"Those were a bad few months," he said. "Then one day Jacob Axley stopped by. I hadn't seen him for several years. He's gone to Illinois to preach. He was in the house only a little while when he said the place was like a morgue. What was the matter with me? he asked. Well, I told him about my idea, about the petition, and why some folks wouldn't sign, and how I didn't know what to do about it.

" 'Did you ask Josh?' he said.

" 'No,' I told him. 'Never thought of that. Besides, I don't want to raise the boy's hopes. Suppose I fail? He'll only be dashed down.'

"Damn if that Jacob didn't let out a great big belly laugh! I wanted to hit him. What was funny about this?

" 'Fletcher,' he says, 'you're no smarter than when I left you. Josh gave you the answer without you even asking him.'

" 'What do you mean?' I said. Then Jacob reached into his pocket and took out a yellowed piece of newspaper. All torn and wrinkled it was, and he smoothes it out gently and says, 'I found this in Garrison's paper. Didn't you ever see it?'

"It was a story about your trial, Josh, and at the end of it, there was what you said to the jury before they sentenced you. Jacob read it out loud to me. I never knew about you saying that. . . . I wanted to copy it out, but Jacob, he made me take it from him. He knew it by heart anyhow, he said. . . . And now, so do I. . . ."

Josh wanted to touch his father, but something

in the stiff, angular figure sitting opposite him forbade it. Then his father looked up, and in his eyes Josh saw a sweet pride he would never forget.

"It made a difference, Josh, knowing what you thought. I saw it all in a different light. I knew you were right in what you had done. And now when I asked people to sign, I wasn't asking a favor for my son. I was asking them to stand up for a man who broke an unjust law and went to prison so other men could be free. It made a difference, all right. Oh, not everyone was convinced. But many more than before. Even those that still said no, they read what you said, and it gave them something to think about."

"What happened with the governor?"

"Nothing at first. I sent him a small batch of petitions but got back only a note saying he'd received them. By then I was seeing lawyers about what to do and how to do it, and of course I was hearing from the Coffins too. They got up petitions, in Ohio—Jacob did in Illinois too—and after a while they spread all around the states out there. New England was our best place, I knew. Lloyd Hawkins had written to me, and I went to see them in Boston. He runs a tailor shop and clothing store there. They got up a whole committee—ministers, lawyers, teachers, businessmen—and the petitions began rolling in. Thousands of people signed, thousands."

He shook his head, as though still marveling that so many strangers could take an interest in what happened to his son.

"I began sending notarized statements of the number of signatures to the governor, and each time I'd ask him if he'd let me bring the petitions in and see you at the same time. It was the same old answer—no. Then when the numbers grew bigger and bigger and lots of important people signed, his office began to say maybe, but wait till the time's right."

"What made it right?"

"The cholera, Josh. Isn't that the damnedest thing? I don't mean the plague by itself, but what you did in the hospital here. The keeper—Mr. Ward—it seems he spoke to the governor—and the governor said all right at last. So I came."

"Pa, you must have spent all your time on this."

His father raised his hand. "Not all, Josh. I still had to keep the farm going."

"If I'd stayed home . . . I could have been helping you all this while."

His father looked at him. "You forget, Josh. I drove you away," he said in a heavy voice.

Josh didn't know how to answer. He felt tears starting to his eyes. "I would have gone sooner or later, Pa. I had to be on my own. It was just a matter of time."

His father nodded. You think what you want, his look seemed to say, I'll think what I have to. They sat there in the late afternoon light, saying nothing now, each thinking about the past. Then his father said, "I've seen the governor already, Josh. I brought him a trunkful of petitions. He said enough time had passed so he could pardon you now. But on one condition. First I have to get the consent of the people who owned Lloyd and Harriet and their child."

"How could you do that? They'd never say yes!"

"You'd be right, son, if you expect them to do it out of the goodness of their hearts. But there's another way. The committee in Boston figured this might happen. The slaveowners will say yes, they told me, if they get paid well enough for it. Lloyd Hawkins dropped everything then, and in sixty days he raised what should be enough money—a good sum, more than the market price would be now. And I'm ready to offer it to them."

Josh's excitement was almost unbearable. "When are you going to see them? Where are they?"

"They're in Lexington now. I'm going there to-morrow."

"You mustn't go, Pa! The cholera's bad there!"

"Not any more. The city's almost clear of it, they tell me."

"But still it's taking a chance. Couldn't you wait?"

"It's the same chance I took coming in here, isn't it?"

His father had been gone about ten days when one morning Josh was taken to the keeper's office.

"Sit down, Bowen," Ward said.

What was wrong? The keeper's voice was strangely solemn.

"I've bad news for you, boy. Your father took sick in Lexington."

"Who's taking care of him? He doesn't know anybody in that place!"

The keeper shifted in his seat. "No need for that now. He's dead. The cholera. Hardly lasted a day after it hit him, they tell me. The authorities had him buried at once."

Josh got up and went over to the window. It was where he had stood next to his father hardly a week ago. He wanted to weep but could not. He had seen nothing of his father for so many years. All the while, he thought they had become strangers. He had done with his life what his father would not have done. Yet in the end it had not diminished the chance of love between them, but strengthened it. And now he was gone. Why couldn't he cry? His feelings seemed frozen deep. But he knew he would begin to miss him more than he had ever let himself feel in the long years since he had left home.

"What will I do now?" he said.

Zeb Ward seemed to know what he meant. "Before he took sick," he said, "he saw those men who owned the Hawkins family and paid them the price. They signed a paper, and your father left it at the governor's office. Matter of fact, it was that same day, on his way back to his rooming house, that he dropped sick right in the street."

"The governor—does he have the papers?"

"He does. You just have to wait."

Three weeks, four weeks, dragged by. At first Josh was terribly restless. He worked feverishly in the weaving room, as though the faster his pace, the sooner he would be free. He had no heart for resuming the Sunday classes, although he knew it would help make the time pass. At night he paced up and down his cell, unable to sleep. As one month turned into two and no word came—had the governor forgotten? who was there to remind him now?—the agitation stopped and a numbness came over him. He would lie on his straw for hours, his eyes blank, his mind suspended. Gradually he became aware of one thought buried in the back of his head. *If I ever get out, I won't do what I did that brought me in here.* It was as though someone else had made a promise. When, he could not tell. He listened to the voice. Not his, it wasn't his, but he would take the advice. He'd done enough, taken his share of the chances; he needed to live, too. His body began to feel lighter. He slept better, ate with an appetite now. A peace settled over his spirit.

When Zeb Ward stopped at his workbench one afternoon, he felt no surprise. Still he trembled all over. Opened his mouth to ask the question, stood there like a man with lockjaw.

"Yes," Ward said, "it came. The pardon from the governor. You can leave tomorrow morning. Just one warning he said to make clear: don't ever come back to Kentucky."

As if they needed to tell me that, he thought. Ward turned away, walked a few steps, then came back. "You don't have to finish the workday," he said. He called a guard to take Josh back to his cell.

He had moved only a few paces when the whole prison seemed to know the news. Nods, smiles, hands waving, lips framing good-bye.

The cell door clanged shut. He sank on his straw, buried his face in his arms and wept.

18

Once More . . .

The prison gates swung open. Josh paused a moment to look back for the last time. The whirring wheels of a sulky clipping down the road distracted him. As it flashed by he caught a glimpse of a young woman driving, her long hair streaming in the wind, her arms raised to whip the horse on. The heavy bolt thudded into place behind him.

The sun burned down, warming the clothes that had come musty and wrinkled from the bag they had been stowed in all these years. A few puffs of white clouds eddied across the blue sky. The summer air was hot and close, but he gulped in great mouthfuls to clean his lungs of the crusted stink of prison.

He had dreamed of this moment many times. To be beyond the walls, out in the open, free to touch grass, flowers, trees. He crossed the dusty road and sat on the grass. He was leaning back against the softness when he snapped erect again. Suppose they changed their minds and put him back in his cell? He got up and walked down the road toward the city.

He had to be out of Kentucky that day by order of the governor. He took the boat at Frankfort and got off in Cincinnati. It was night when he knocked at the Coffins' door. Kate opened it and in the weak light had trouble seeing who it was. He was much thinner, his eyes reddened from the constant smoke of the lamps, his skin a chalky white. But in a moment she knew him and put her arms around him. He could feel her tears against his cheek. Levi shook his hand violently, and began asking him a hundred questions before Kate made him stop.

They wanted him to sit down to supper. But first he had to walk around the room. Not a cell. A room. Sofa, armchair, rocker, scatter rugs, clean walls. And the table, with cloth laid, and sparkling dishes. He picked up books on the shelves, fingered the pages.

At last he could sit down. It was hard to say anything. He looked up at them, his eyes asking to be let alone. Kate reached over and put her hand on his.

That night he slept as though he had dropped into the center of a huge sweet-smelling hayrick. It was early afternoon before he woke. He soaked in a hot tub for an hour, then put on the new clothes Levi had got for him that morning.

In the evening friends came over, the antislavery old guard—Henry Boyd, William Watson, Samuel Lewis, Salmon Chase. They talked quietly of politics and abolition, careful not to press him to say anything. After a while he found himself joining in with questions. And before the night was over, he was struggling for words to tell them what the years away had been like. He would only speak of what others did and of how they looked. His feelings about himself were too dangerous. They did not know what he had promised himself those last weeks in prison.

When the others left, Levi said he must tell everyone about his experiences in Kentucky. Not only the prison, but what he had learned of slavery. "They will want to know," he said. "The movement can arrange public meetings. And people will come."

"Yes," Kate said, "but not now. He needs to rest a while." Josh looked at her gratefully.

He went for long walks, watched the ships on the river, attended a concert. Levi brought him newspapers to read, but he was not ready for that yet. Instead he buried himself in Scott and Dickens and James Fenimore Cooper. He listened when Levi and Kate talked about the movement, but he took no part in it. It felt remote to him. They sensed his distance but thought it best not to ask why. In a few weeks, as word got around that he was free, letters came asking him to speak at antislavery meetings. Reluctantly, he said yes, feeling uneasy at Levi's enthusiasm.

It was the small towns first. He wanted to get used to being on his feet again, in front of an audience. Then Cleveland and Detroit, where there were great seas of faces staring up at him. The crowds were eager, impatient to know every detail. In the old days when he was on the circuit he would have thrilled to their keenness, but now he sweated and trembled. He wanted to run. The great hall would tilt before his eyes, the faces dim and blur, the floor slip beneath his feet. But the thunder of thousands of hands clapping kept him going. After each speech men and women would wait in line to shake his hand. In some eyes he saw awe, in others pity. He wanted neither—only to escape the unrelenting attention.

The audiences no longer were a challenge. They seemed to agree with him before he said anything. He went wherever he liked, and when sometimes they tried to pay him more than for his expenses, he grew angry. This was not his job, his work. What was? he wondered. He hated the hero worship. It made him feel false.

Gradually his speeches lost any edge. He would hear his own voice as though it were a stranger speaking, a man saying the same thing too often, with all true feeling gone. He could sense the audience slipping away from him, their minds adrift, their eyes no longer fixed on him. Sometimes an unreasoning anger would rise in him, anger at them. Where were they when he was in prison. . . . What did they do but go to a meeting, write a letter, sign a petition. . . . His words did little but stir their sentimental feelings. And then they would go home, he knew, enjoy themselves for a moment as they repeated one of his adventure stories and by bedtime forget it all.

Moving through southern Indiana on a tour, he suddenly took off for Louisville. As soon as he crossed over into Kentucky he felt better. He walked the city streets, looking into faces, wondering if anyone would recognize him. He saw no one he knew. The town was full of small operators now, men who mixed slave-trading with money-lending and real estate deals and the peddling of miscellaneous merchandise. He found himself heading for the big slave markets. At Matthew Garrison's—it was a foolish thing to do, but the fact that a slave dealer had the same name as the hated abolitionist editor intrigued him—he went inside. He strolled around the yard, pretending to be looking for bargains among the young men and women Garrison advertised for "refined domestic work."

He stayed in the city only for the day, and that night was back in Jeffersonville, the village on the Indiana side of the river. The next day a man came to see him, sent on by Levi Coffin. He wanted to ask Josh's advice on how best to go about the rescue of a young Louisville slave called Tamar, who wanted to escape. They sat there in his room, discussing all the particulars of Tamar's situation. Josh went over the details needed to work out a plan.

"Who'll do it?" he asked when they were through.

The man hesitated. "We don't know yet," he said. "We have one or two people in mind. I think it will be decided as soon as I get back with this plan."

"No need for that," said Josh. "I'll do it."

He had said it without stopping to think. The words seemed to come out of his mouth by themselves. The man looked delighted. "That would be perfect," he said. "But we didn't intend to ask you. After all . . ."

"After all what? I know how. I'm here. Then why not?"

The man did not argue. He needed a day, he said, to pass the information to Tamar. "She'll be ready," he said. "Unless you hear from me, cross over to Louisville the day after tomorrow."

The agent slipped out, and Josh went to bed. He fell asleep with no trouble. About four in the morning he started awake, frightened. Until daylight came he could not get his mind off the prison at Frankfort. All the while he had been discussing plans for someone else to rescue Tamar, he had coolly calculated risks, like an exercise in mathematics. But in sleep the fear took over and would not let go. It was only six months since he had got out of prison. Why had he volunteered? What reason did he have to pick up the burden again? And when others stood ready to do it? But nothing could go wrong this time. Louisville sat on the opposite shore of the Ohio, and all he had to do was to take Tamar across the river and they would be on free soil. It would not be hard. The plan was so simple there was nothing to go wrong.

On Sunday morning he took the ferry over the Ohio and walked to the Baptist church of which Tamar was a member. He timed it so that he arrived just before services were to end. When the congregation came out the door, he stood across the street and watched. Tamar, a frail nineteen-year-old, who had been carefully described to him, came down the steps talking with some friends. If she was able to carry out the prearranged plan, she would be holding a blue kerchief in her hand. If not, the color would be red.

It was blue. He noticed her eyes studying people on the street until they paused on him and met his eyes. Then she moved away with her friends. He gave no sign and walked off in the opposite direction.

The blue signal meant she had a pass from her master to visit a friend that evening. She must be home by ten, for any slave found on the streets after that hour was taken to the watchhouse and whipped.

At nine he was at the foot of a road on the northeast side of town which led to the riverbank. He hid in some bushes, and a few minutes later Tamar appeared out of the dark. He whistled a prearranged birdcall, and she came over and crouched beside him. She had nothing with her but the clothes she wore and a dove-colored shawl she prized. He learned she was leaving no one behind. She had been separated by sale from her parents many years before. Now her owner, Mr. Shotwell, needed cash and was putting her in Matthew Garrison's hands for sale south.

Josh had been able to find only a leaky old skiff to take them across the river. It was so full of holes he had brought along a tin cup for bailing. While Tamar knelt on the bottom, scooping out the water that came in steadily, he used a board to propel the skiff toward the Indiana shore. Every few minutes he had to put aside the makeshift oar and cup his hands to help her get rid of the water that threatened to sink them. Almost inch by inch, they moved toward the far shore.

The skiff began spinning around in a mad circle, caught in a whirlpool made by logs snagged on rocks beneath the surface. He thought they were done for. Tamar dropped the cup and began to cry. "Damn!" he yelled, grabbing for the cup before it could wash overboard. Holding it between his teeth he paddled furiously. He could not force the skiff out of the whirling circle. His hands were raw and bleeding from the effort, and his breathing came in great gasps. Just then a stray log which had floated into the whirlpool struck against the side so heavily that it shoved the light skiff out of the danger zone. Dizzy and vomiting, Tamar managed to begin bailing again, and he bent to his paddle. They were soaked to the skin and shivering from the icy water. He felt his muscles tighten and feared a cramp might seize arm or leg. Now he could see the low trees overhanging the Indiana bank. It was about forty yards away. But the skiff had shipped so much water it was like pushing against lead to make it move. He decided they would try to swim the rest of the distance. He was so exhausted he was not at all sure he could make it.

"Can you swim?" he asked.

"A little."

"I'll swim on my back," he said, "and hold you above me. If we both keep kicking, we'll make shore."

He rolled out of the skiff, and helped Tamar out. They started. Every scissoring of his legs was agony. They made poor progress. Then it was better for twenty yards or so, until a savage cramp gripped his right leg. "Can't go on," he gasped in her ear. "Cramps. Go it yourself!"

"Float," she said, "I'll push." She turned on to her belly, floundered behind him till she got a grip on his shoulders, then kicking out, tried to shove him in to shore. She was too slight to make much headway against his weight and the water. "Let go!" he yelled frantically. "Swim in yourself!" She said nothing, kept pushing, and as if by a miracle he felt his body twist abruptly to the left, then shoot right toward the riverbank. Her grip on him was broken, but she too was thrust in the same direction. They had been caught up in a swift current running toward the shore and in a few moments were carried in. His back scraped sandy bottom, and he knew they were safe.

They lay there in the shallows, their arms around each other, unable to get up. The water lapped quietly over them. If he could only fall asleep and never have to wake. Through the branches above them he could see the sky growing pale. They had to be under cover before daylight would reveal them to anyone on the opposite shore. She got to her knees, supporting him, and they crawled up the riverbank. They staggered painfully downshore a short way to a cave under the bank, where he had hidden food and a change of clothing for both of them. They rested there, hardly able to talk. He felt like a sponge that had soaked up water for years. Touch him at any point and he thought he would run like a spring. Around midday he grew hot and trembly and feared a fever was coming on. Tamar bathed his face in the cool river water and he fell asleep. When she woke him gently late in the afternoon, the illness was gone.

At nightfall he left Tamar and walked to nearby Jeffersonville, where he hired a horse and buggy, using the name of King. Then he drove back to the river and picked up Tamar. Now she was wearing dark clothes, a straw bonnet, and a green veil. They set out on the road to Salem, about thirty miles distant.

The buggy bumped along the rough road. It was about nine o'clock when a wheel sank into a deep rut and the axle cracked from the shock. They could not go on without repairs. Josh lit a lantern and found a house about a quarter mile off the road. The farmer agreed to bring some tools and help fix the buggy. When they came back to Tamar, Josh introduced her as his wife, Mrs. King. He said they lived in Jeffersonville and were headed for Salem where they meant to catch a train. The farmer refused to take any money for his help. Josh thanked him and they got under way again.

At Salem he put her aboard the train. When it reached Vincennes, he told her, she would be met by the abolitionist agent who had worked out the rescue with Josh. He wanted to embrace her—he owed her his life—but caution kept him to a casual wave of the hand.

Josh drove back to Jeffersonville. He felt good, though bone-tired. Another day, and it would be time to leave for his next meeting. He went to bed early and slept until midmorning. After breakfast, he walked out for some air. He was passing the stable from which he had hired the horse and buggy when the owner called out to him. He walked over. When he stepped through the door three men moved out of the shadows and asked the stableman, "Is this the man?"

"Yes," the stableman answered.

One of the men stepped forward and said to Josh, "I want you."

"What do you want of me?"

"They want you in Louisville," the man said. "You been aiding off some niggers."

"I won't come! Who are you? Only an Indiana court can order a man in this state to be given up to Kentucky. What authority do you have?"

"Authority, hell," he said. "I'm a Kentucky marshal." He grabbed Josh by the collar, put his hand inside and twisted the collar to choke him. Josh found it hard to speak or even breathe. Then one of the other men took hold of his arms. Josh kicked him in the knee, shoved his elbow into the other man's ribs, but now the third man piled on him. He resisted with all his might, but they soon had him pinned to the floor of the stable. He yelled for help. A man passing on the street stopped, looked in the door, shrugged and went on. The three men sat on him while the stable owner hurried off. Soon he was back with a man who said he was the sheriff. He ordered Josh to be taken to jail. "But what am I guilty of?" he protested. "These men have no right to take me."

"You come along peaceable," said the sheriff, "and we'll find out about that." Josh agreed to go quietly. But as they walked along, the Kentucky marshal dropped behind with the sheriff and whispered intently to him for a few minutes. The sheriff then moved up and said, "Here, this man has pledged to take responsibility for you." And to Josh's astonishment, he began to walk off, leaving him in the hands of the kidnappers. Josh shouted after the sheriff, accused him of taking a bribe, but the man paid no heed. The Kentuckians hurried Josh to the river and, not risking the wait for a ferry, shoved him into a small boat, tying his hands and feet. In minutes they had rowed him far out on the river, beyond rescue.

Landing on the Kentucky side, they put irons on his wrists and ankles and fastened a long chain from one set to the other. Then they hoisted him on to a wagon and drove him to the Louisville courthouse. There he was searched and asked his name. He refused to answer any questions.

The marshal grinned at him. "Don't matter," he said. "We know. Joshua Bowen, the little ole nigger-stealer." He led Josh out of the courtroom and down a flight of steps to a block of cells beneath the courtrooms. He unlocked one and pushed the prisoner inside. Josh stumbled in the deep shadows, felt clumsily for a bench and sat down. The marshal stood outside, peering through the bars at him, one hand holding a lantern high.

"Rest easy, boy," he said. "Take a whole army of nigger-stealers to get you outa here."

Afterword:
On History and Fiction

Readers often ask how a historical novel is created. How much of it is fact and how much fiction? How are they linked? Or they may ask, what is "true" and what is "untrue"? I would answer by saying that if a novel is good, the truth of it exists quite apart from verifiable facts—which doesn't mean, at least in the case of *Underground Man*, that most of the story isn't taken from history.

Sometimes I've been asked, Why did you choose to make a white rather than a black the hero of your novel? At the time I began the book, there were in print several biographies for young people of black abolitionists—people like Harriet Tubman, Frederick Douglass, Sojourner Truth. There were very few about white abolitionists, however, even such prominent ones as William Lloyd Garrison or Wendell Phillips, and none at all about white abolitionists, such as Calvin Fairbank, who dared go into the South to rescue slaves. Surely they deserved to have their stories told? Especially since the white rescuers were few indeed compared to the number of whites who either openly favored slavery or may have disliked it but kept silent and did nothing. Most slaves who escaped had only themselves and their fellow blacks to thank.

I find a kind of parallel between telling stories such as Fairbank's and telling the story of the very small minority of Christians who risked their lives to rescue Jews during the Nazi era. In my book *Rescue: The Story of the Gentiles Who Saved Jews during the Holocaust,* I said: "Against the immense darkness of the Holocaust, the light shone by the rescuers is only a tiny flicker." But those few, like Calvin Fairbank or my fictional hero, Josh Bowen, were men and women whose lives were witness to the truth that there *is* an alternative to the passive acceptance of evil. It was Fairbank's—or Josh's—ability to respond to the evil of slavery that made his attempts at rescue possible. He felt compassion for the suffering of others, strangers though they were, and so he acted, bound in the oneness of humanity.

Underground Man was my first work of fiction. It came after twenty years of writing nonfiction, chiefly history and biography. And it didn't begin as a novel, but as a biography of Calvin Fairbank. I had run across his name in several books about the antislavery movement. Brief as the references to his courage and daring were, they intrigued me. What had he been like? Where had he come from? What forces had shaped his character and led him south to rescue black men, women, and children from slavery?

To answer these questions I set out to write his biography. But because my research failed to unearth enough evidence to do justice to his story, I decided reluctantly to give it up. Then an editor suggested that I write a novel about the man instead. After all, I had written many books about African American history and the antislavery movement; couldn't I use that experience to create a fictional image of Fairbank?

Challenged by the prospect of trying a new form of writing, I agreed. I soon discovered that because I had begun by using Fairbank's real name, I felt blocked in my efforts to imagine characters, events, and dialogue that were not strictly according to the actual facts. In short, it was my training as a historian that inhibited me. Then one night, waking from sleep, I saw the solution as though written in the air before me. Why not change the hero's name? And so he became Joshua Bowen, instead of Calvin

Fairbank, which removed the barrier to invention. Josh was *my* creation. I could put ideas in his head, words in his mouth, and feelings in his heart that sprang from my own understanding of such a man's character and temperament.

My venture into fiction was not at the expense of history, however. Almost everything in the novel is solidly rooted in fact. I collected data like an investigative reporter (which is one aspect of the historian's job). On my shelves were rows of books about African American history and the abolition movement, gathered in the course of research for previous projects. My desk was piled high with notes when a lucky find occurred. In a secondhand book-store (I am always prowling them for such treasures) I found a blue-covered book, cheaply printed and now almost in tatters, dated 1890. The title page read, *"Rev. Calvin Fairbank during Slavery Times"* and, below it, "Edited from the manuscript." A brief preface by Fairbank stated that he had written a 1,200-page manuscript, "but everyone considered it too long." He had then cut it to the bone.

It was a great break, though I raged against those well-meaning friends—probably tired of hearing his tales of adventure—who had made him throw away much the bigger part of the story. Fairbank writes in a plain style, simple, direct, and with a fierce hatred of slavery sizzling just below the surface. Sometimes he recalls conversations and provides character sketches of the people he encountered in his struggle to liberate slaves. But there are holes in the story, gaps any reader would want to have filled in. "And *then* what happened?"—always in the avid reader's mind when pursuing an adventure story. I also wanted to know more about the places his adventures took him to, about the people who tried to help him or hurt him, and about the experience of being imprisoned for long years.

Because I was writing for young readers, I changed the time sequence of the story, thereby making my hero about ten years younger than he actually was at the time of these events. I thought by doing that I would enable my readers to identify more readily with the hero. But except for that change, almost everything in the book is true. The people he encounters derive from the people Fairbank knew; they bear their actual names. Although some of the dialogue is adapted from Fairbank's own account, more of it is invented by me—consistent, I hope, with how people in that time saw themselves and understood the issues.

Fairbank's autobiography dismisses his childhood in a few pages. We learn very little about his family, his parents, their feelings for one another.

(These may have been given much more attention in the original draft.) What I decided to do, then, was to conjure up a family life for him, to imagine relationships and interests that might influence the development of a boy born in the wilderness of upstate New York in the early nineteenth century.

Because I particularly wanted a dramatic opening to hook the reader and at the same time express the tension between a father and his son, I hit upon the bear hunt in Chapter 1. Jacob Axley, a fictional character, is based on what I'd read of circuit preachers on the frontier—their goals, their duties, the hardships of their ministry, the rewards of their work. Gradually Josh finds himself moving toward preaching. His need for a new birth in Christ comes from Fairbank's own book, in which he mourns his youthful alienation from God and from time to time promises himself resignation to His will. Fairbank wrote that often, alone in the forest, he would imagine himself with an audience before him, "pointing them to the lamb of God."

In Chapter 4 the description of the revival meeting in the campground is derived from many books I read about the Great Awakening that seized America in that time. The classic source for the connection between religious revival and antislavery is Gilbert H. Barnes, *The Anti-Slavery Impulse*,

1830–1844 (1933). God, the preachers said, insisted that the saved perform benevolent deeds, that they take a personal responsibility for improving society. Out of such a spirit sprang the crusade against slavery. Young people like Fairbank began to see social activism as a way of life. Some became circuit riders, abolition agents, editors of radical papers—burning to aid in America's regeneration.

When I write about Jacob Axley preaching to the vast crowd, his words are taken from reports I read about other preachers. The books in the saddlebags that form Josh's schooling were actually read at the time. I took special pleasure in putting in Lydia Maria Child's abolitionist "Appeal"; I had just written a biography of Mrs. Child and was very fond of this feisty woman who fought so hard against slavery and for women's rights.

The episode of Josh's encounter with the runaway slave Sam, which takes up most of chapters 5 and 6, runs less than two pages in the Fairbank book. But it was enough to get me going, to give me a chance to re-create Sam's life as a slave on a Kentucky farm as he tells it to Josh. The details of his story I took in part from the many authentic narratives of fugitive slaves published in the pre–Civil War years to win support for the abolitionist cause. I took passages from Solomon Northup's *Twelve*

Years a Slave (1853) and the *Narrative of the Life of Frederick Douglass* (1845) as well as from other slave tales for my documentary books *The Black Americans: A History in Their Own Words* (1964, 1985). The narratives were powerful portraits of slave life, of physical abuse and privation, of separation from loved ones, of emotional distress. They gave Northern whites a vivid picture of the slaves' humanity, their cultural vitality, and their accomplishments, thus undermining current racial myths. In my novel the effect of his meeting with Sam is to waken in Josh the determination to identify himself with the people "that are in bonds, as bound with them."

In Chapter 7, Josh crosses the Ohio to Kentucky to start his new and dangerous life as an agent of the Underground Railroad. It was in this slave state that most of Fairbank's daring rescues took place. To build my knowledge of the conditions of slavery there, of the attitudes of both whites and blacks, I read several books about the Kentucky of that day. Most useful was J. Winston Coleman's *Slavery Times in Kentucky* (1940). I had used it earlier while researching other books but now found it enormously helpful for both details and insights. It contains many references to Fairbank himself. Some of what Fairbank's own book tells us is supplemented and enriched by fresh information Coleman gathered from contemporary newspapers and court records. Coleman's bibliography steered me to other books and pamphlets about the state's slave conditions as well as to biographies of Kentuckians.

The personality of Reverend Billy Shaw and the description of the miserable farm he operates near Maysville (Chapter 7) are alike taken from the accounts of travelers in the South. Many Europeans visited the slave states and, returning home, published their impressions. Americans from the free states did the same. One of the most valued accounts is by the New Englander Frederick Law Olmsted, who made two lengthy trips south between 1852 and 1854, reporting his day-to-day observations for a New York newspaper. The assignment resulted in three volumes that later appeared as *The Cotton Kingdom* (1861). The same Olmsted became the nation's foremost landscape architect, designing New York City's Central Park and many other parks and gardens.

Shaw's slave Annie is depicted partly out of imagination and partly from vignettes of tough-minded women who never let a master enslave their spirit. The elements of Shaw's sermon to the slave congregation came from travelers' accounts of sermons they sat through while visiting plantations.

The Quaker Levi Coffin, introduced into the story in Chapter 8, is a major historical figure with whom Fairbank worked early on. In his role as "president" of the Underground Railroad, Coffin helped thousands of slaves to freedom. The Society of Friends, also known as Quakers, was the first religious institution in this country to condemn slavery as morally evil and the first to require all its members to free their slaves. They helped to found antislavery organizations and did much to advance the restriction on or ending of slavery. Many Quakers probably would have quietly aided fugitives who came to their doors, but some, like Coffin, became organizers of rescue attempts.

I found much useful material in histories of the rescue movement. They included Larry Gara, *The Liberty Line: The Legend of the Underground Railroad* (1961); Wilbur H. Siebert, *The Underground Railroad from Slavery to Freedom* (1898); and William Still, *The Underground Railroad: A Record of Facts, Authentic Narratives, Letters, Etc.* (1872). Still, a free black, was a leader of underground railroad operations in Pennsylvania from 1849 to 1861 and was involved in many of the most famous rescue cases. His is the source closest to actual history.

Josh's talk with Levi Coffin expresses the views of most Quakers, considered moderates by such abolitionists as William Lloyd Garrison, who advocated immediate emancipation and denounced the Constitution as a slave document. When Coffin convinces Josh to attend the school in New York for the training of antislavery agents, it gives me the chance to show what this intense form of special education devoted to a cause was like. (There were similar schools in the 1960s, to train college students to go south and help in the civil rights movement.) All the people brought into the story here are historical figures: Theodore Weld, William Lloyd Garrison, the Grimke sisters, Amos Dresser—about whom or by whom much has been written. Benjamin Thomas's biography, *Theodore Weld, Crusader for Freedom* (1950), describes the school.

Fairbank did not attend the New York school, but he did study at Oberlin College, an Ohio school considered radical because it offered, for the first time in the history of higher education, equal instruction to men, women, and blacks. Fairbank must have met antislavery students and teachers there.

The tactics antislavery agents used—to enter churches and without permission stand up and speak boldly against slavery, and often against the church itself for its silence on the issue—is dramatized in Chapter 9. My knowledge of these tactics comes from the memoirs of such men as Henry C. Wright,

Stephen Foster, and Parker Pillsbury as well as from reports of their actions in the *Liberator*, Garrison's newspaper. They were called "come-outers," because they advocated separation from their slaveholding brethren. They were tossed out, beaten, and nearly lynched for the uproar they caused in church. Quotes from press clippings and the placards reproduced in the book are all authentic. After exposure to a series of these, Josh decides that his work must be in the South itself. He can't wait for emancipation. He must act now to help free slaves. He thinks not in abstract numbers—millions of people in bondage—but of individuals, of real men and women and children. The conversation he has with Levi Coffin, considering whether to go disguised as a peddler (a common front) or as the circuit rider he himself was, is based on the tactics men like him used.

The story of William Minnis (Chapter 9) is given by Fairbank in considerable detail; Emily Ward's and the Rhoads' stories, much less so. Helen Payne occupies only a paragraph in Fairbank's book, but I saw the opportunity to enrich her story with an attempt to get at her thinking. Kentucky's pressure on Ohio to stop interfering with slave property is in the official records of both states. I introduce other rescue efforts, such as Julie's story (Chapter 10), to illustrate how masters sexually exploited their female slaves, even those as young as Julie. The horrifying outcome of Julie's attempt to escape demonstrates the great risk of flight.

The last part of Chapter 10 and all of Chapter 11 focus on the story of Talitha and the slave question. It was the "most extraordinary incident" in Fairbank's life, he says in his book. He gives about eight pages to it. Coleman's history of Kentucky devotes four pages to the Eliza auction; I found it took me twenty pages to tell it the way I wished. I changed the woman's real name from Eliza to Talitha because I invented a few of the details. The Noah Tyler episode is purely fictional but based on accounts of slave auctions in the newspapers of the period.

Salmon P. Chase and Nicholas Longworth, who played important roles in backing Talitha's—or Eliza's—purchase, were important historical figures. Chase, an abolitionist lawyer, later became Senator from Ohio, governor of the state, Lincoln's Secretary of the Treasury, and Chief Justice of the U.S. Supreme Court. Longworth was a noted horticulturist.

Josh's encounter with Deborah Walker (Chapter 12) is based on the connection between Fairbank and a Vermont woman, Delia A. Webster, the head of a school for girls in Lexington, Kentucky. I changed her name and some of the circumstances to suit my plot, but the basic story is true. Coleman's history tells us much more about it than Fairbank does, many of his details taken from reports in the Kentucky press and from court records.

The rescue of the Lloyd Hawkins family by Deborah and Josh stands upon the actual rescue by Webster and Fairbank of Lewis Hayden, his wife, and their son. The family ultimately reached Boston, where Hayden became one of the busiest station-keepers on the Underground Railroad, helping runaways and gaining considerable influence in Boston as a leader in the black community. The John Rankin who takes over the protection of the Hawkins family on the free side of the Ohio was a well-known white abolitionist originally from the South.

The arrest of Josh and Deborah is exactly as it happened. My account of the trial is taken from the press, court records, and a pamphlet published by Webster herself, which contains some of the documents I quote from. The differences between their positions gave me a chance to probe the crisis of conscience both people faced as they decided on a course of action. Josh's speech to the court before sentencing I made up out of my sense of what such abolitionists felt and how they reasoned. Fairbank provides only a few sentences about it in his memoir.

Life in the Kentucky prison (Chapters 14–17) is touched on only briefly by Fairbank. But starting from the elementary facts, I was able to enlarge on them after much research. I found that Dorothea Dix, the social reformer who crusaded for more humane treatment of the mentally ill and the imprisoned, had visited the prison during the years Fairbank was there. Her long report of neglect and abuse, of what the cells looked like, how the prisoners were treated, and the work they were made to do was invaluable.

But how reconstruct the mental and emotional state of Josh in prison? What was it like for a notorious abolitionist to be thrown among prisoners, most of whom hated what he stood for? I thought of other prisoners whose dissident points of view must have alienated them from their fellow inmates. I remembered reading the prison memoirs of Alexander Berkman, the anarchist who spent twenty years in a Pennsylvania penitentiary for his attempt to kill Henry Clay Frick, the manager of the Carnegie steelworks, because of Frick's brutality to the workers during the Homestead strike of 1892. Rereading his book and looking up the memoirs of other political prisoners helped me to put myself in Josh's place.

The details about the weaving of hemp in prison came from Fairbank's book. He was actually allowed to conduct Sunday school classes and to preach in prison. I invented his use of newspaper stories that recorded aspects of Southern life, but the clippings themselves are all real. A cholera epidemic did strike Kentucky at the time and spread to the prison, but Fairbank gives it only a paragraph. I built it up to dramatize the compassionate side of Josh's character and to bring his recovery of faith and hope to a climax.

Fairbank's father really did come to Kentucky to carry petitions for his son's release and was struck down by the plague and buried among strangers. I used Josh's meeting in prison with his father and their reconciliation to bring on the final resolution of the conflict between the two that set the story going in my opening chapter.

Fairbank, like Josh, was pardoned after nearly five years in prison. And, like Fairbank, Josh goes on a tour (Chapter 18), speaking at antislavery meetings. And again, like Fairbank, Josh while in Indiana responds to an appeal to rescue Tamar, a slave about to be sold on the auction block. The rescue accomplished, Fairbank was kidnapped on free soil and forced back into Kentucky, where he was convicted for violation of the slave code. Fairbank was sentenced to fifteen years at hard labor.

My story ends with the slamming of the prison door behind Josh. I wrote this note to let readers know that the story of Josh was fundamentally true. Fairbank himself stayed in that prison until the Civil War, when Union troops entered Kentucky and freed him. He spent seventeen years behind bars.

Milton Meltzer has authored over eighty books for young people, mostly consisting of biographies and historical nonfiction. He is a recipient of the Christopher Award and the Jane Addams Children's Book Award, among other honors. He has been nominated for the National Book Award five times. Mr. Meltzer lives in New York City.